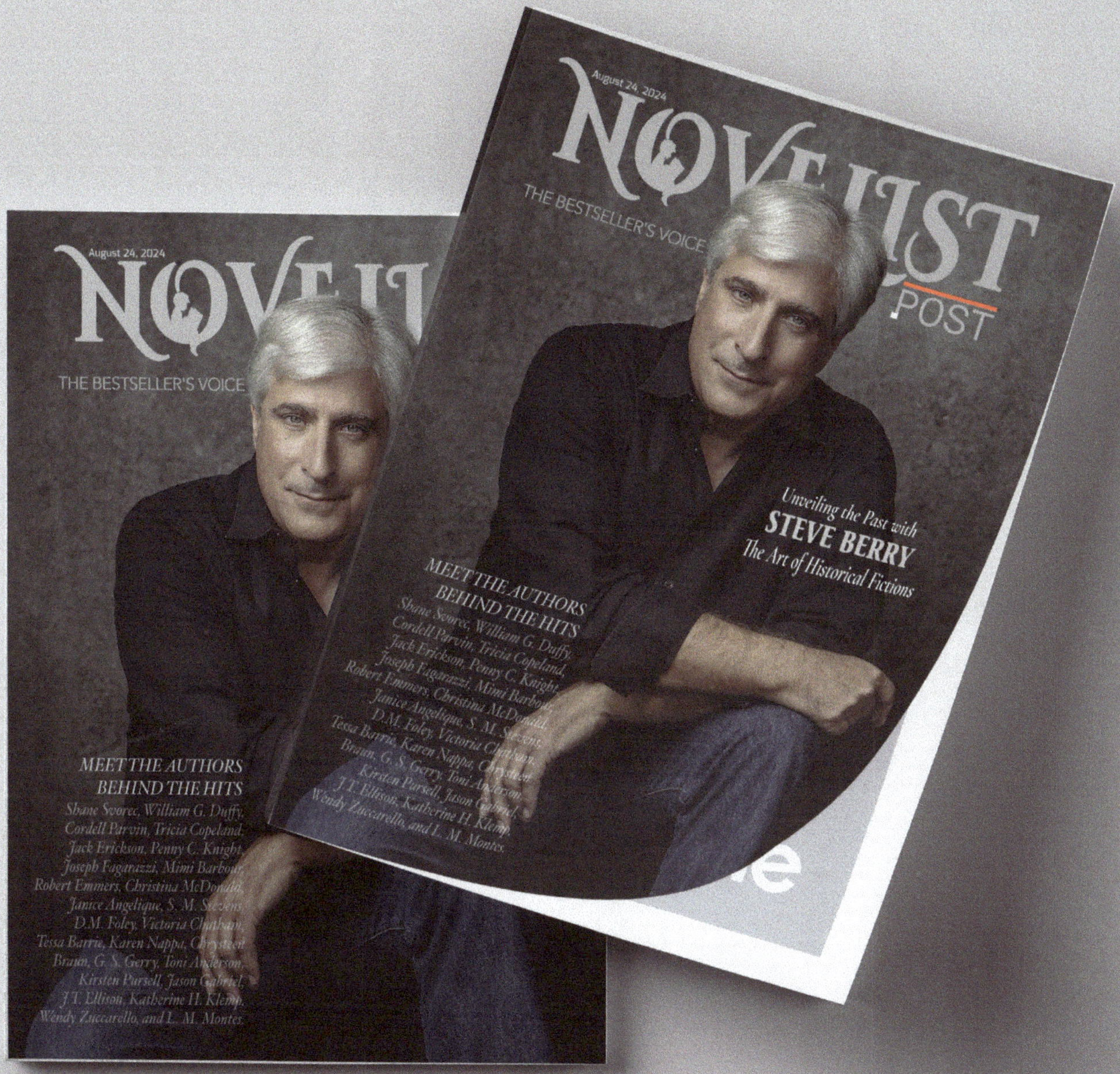

Available on

amazon

FICTION FAVORITES

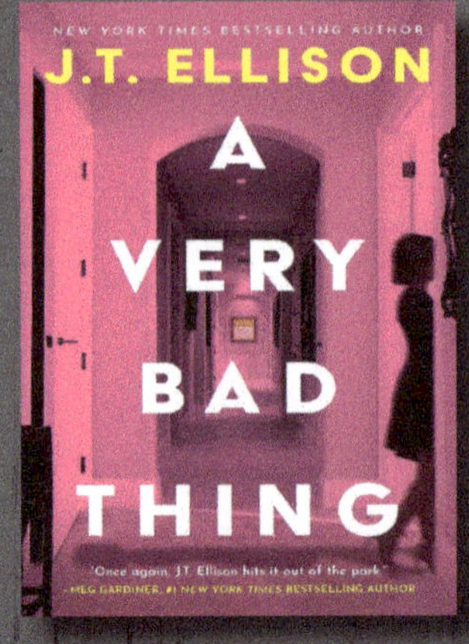

All We Ever Wanted
EMILY GIFFIN

Page-turning . . . Timely and thought-provoking, it's Giffin's best yet."
—People

https://amzn.to/3WNATEc

A Very Bad Thing
J.T. ELLISON

"A Very Bad Thing is a wonderfully smart, twisty psychological thriller infused with dark secrets, high drama, and edgy tension. Wow, what a ride!"
—Jayne Ann Krentz, New York Times bestselling author

https://amzn.to/4c41ktK

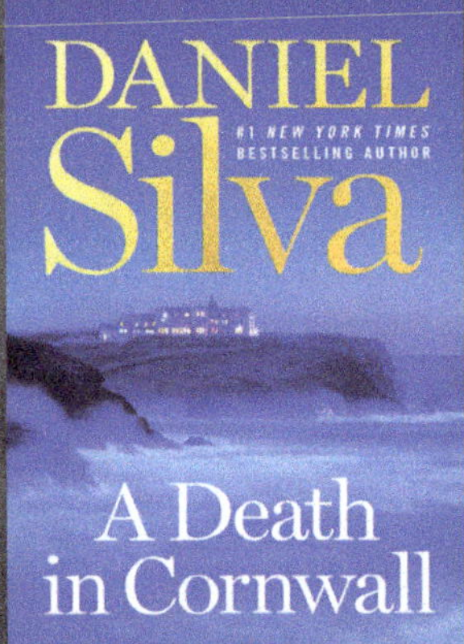

A Death in Cornwall
DANIEL SILVA

"Vastly entertaining with a blend of familiar characters, unrivaled plot development acumen, and artful repartee"
— J McIver

https://amzn.to/3WPoOyx

The Lions of Fifth Avenue
FIONA DAVIS

"The Lions of Fifth Avenue is a book written for booklovers."
—O, The Oprah Magazine

https://amzn.to/3LPu7al

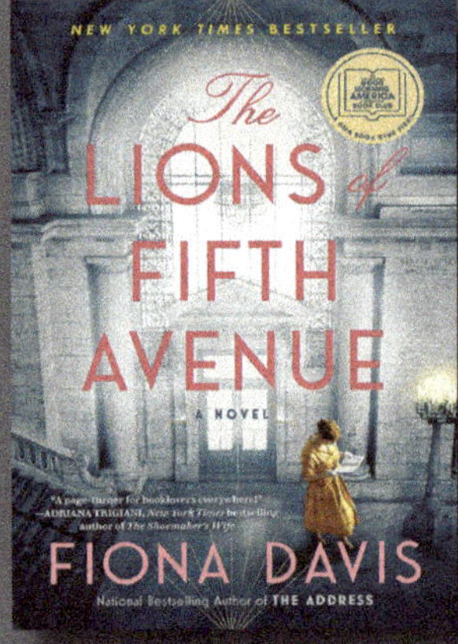

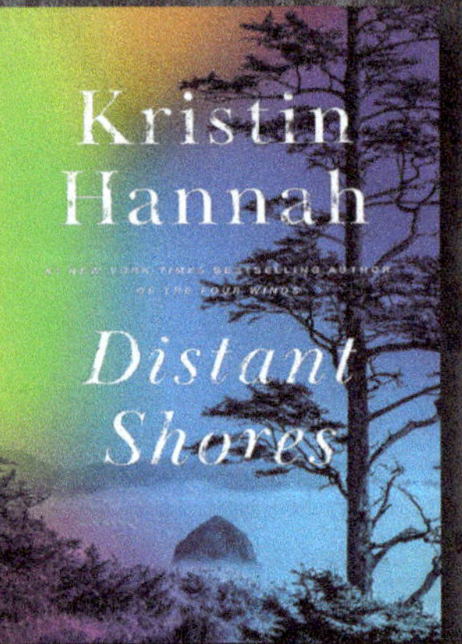

Distant Shores
KRISTIN HANNAH

"Certain to strike a chord . . . winning characterizations . . . and a few surprises."
—The Seattle Times

https://amzn.to/4d8uuco

Sandwich
CATHERINE NEWMAN

"If you want a book that has you from 'hello,' this is the one."
— Ann Patchett, PBS NewsHour

https://amzn.to/3yb2shu

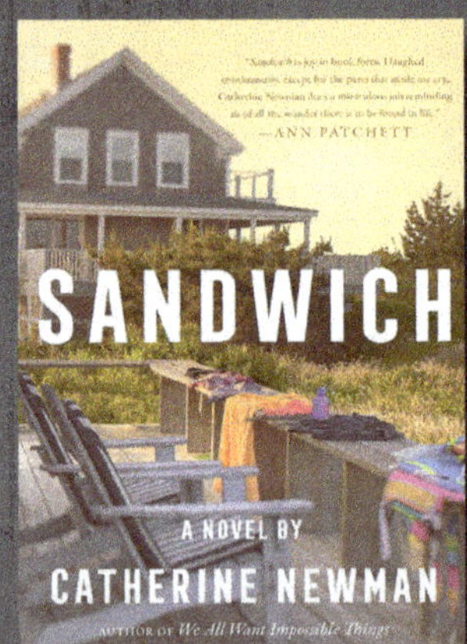

The Book of Lost Friends
LISA WINGATE

"A [story] of a family lost and found . . . a poignant, engrossing tale about sibling love and the toll of secrets."
—People

https://amzn.to/3WmZIoY

Clete
JAMES LEE BURKE

"James Lee Burke is the reigning champ of nostalgia noir."
—New York Times Book Review

https://amzn.to/3LMAlmv

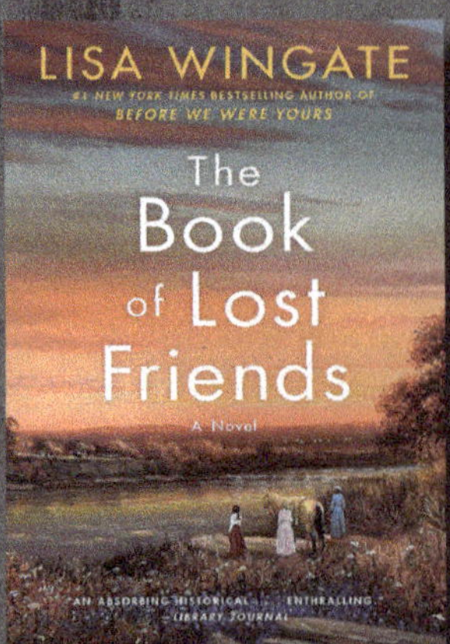

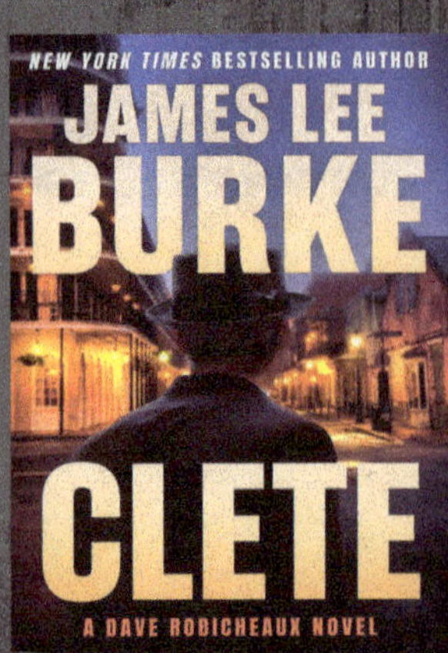

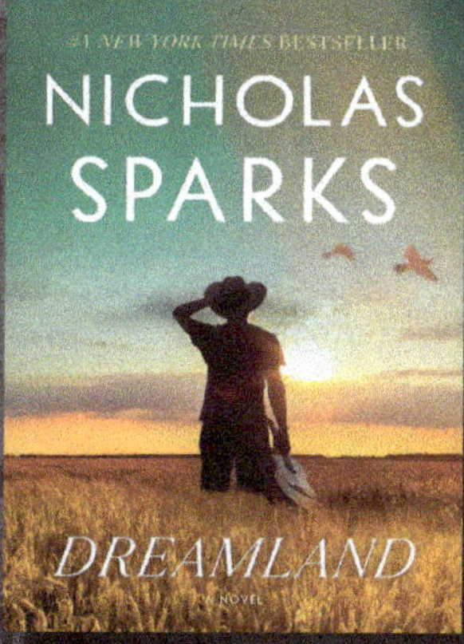

Dreamland
NICHOLAS SPARKS

"From this singular work it's clear that [Sparks] . . . continues to hone his craft."
—The Cullman Times

https://amzn.to/3Yx5tTR

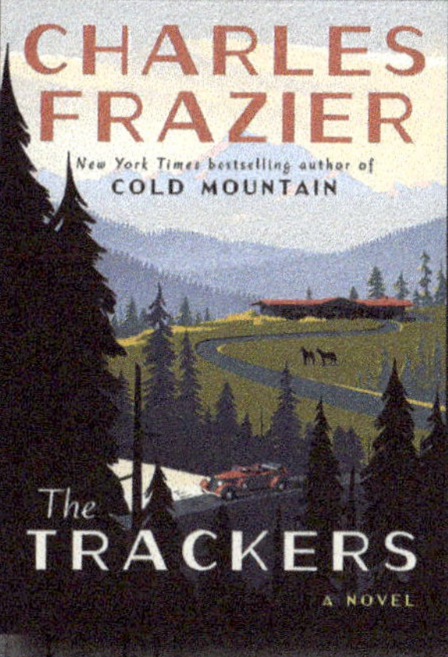

The Trackers
CHARLES FRAZIER

"Frazier is in top form…. Period-authentic, and the writing hums with spectacular word-images…. [A] propulsive tale of individualistic characters striving to beat the odds."

— Booklist (starred review)

https://amzn.to/3WwTWRJ

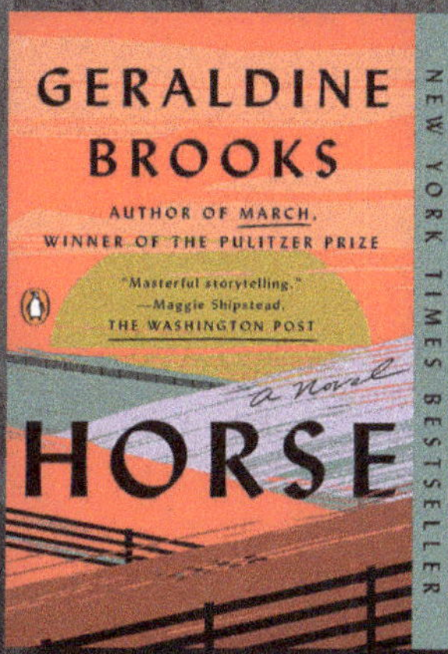

Horse
GERALDINE BROOKS

"[A] deft novel . . . create[s] a picture of the artistic, athletic, and scientific passions that horses can inspire in humans."
—The New Yorker

https://amzn.to/4d6exne

The Girl Who Survived
LISA JACKSON

This suspenseful thriller is packed with jaw-dropping twists."
—InTouch

https://amzn.to/3A0VUlR

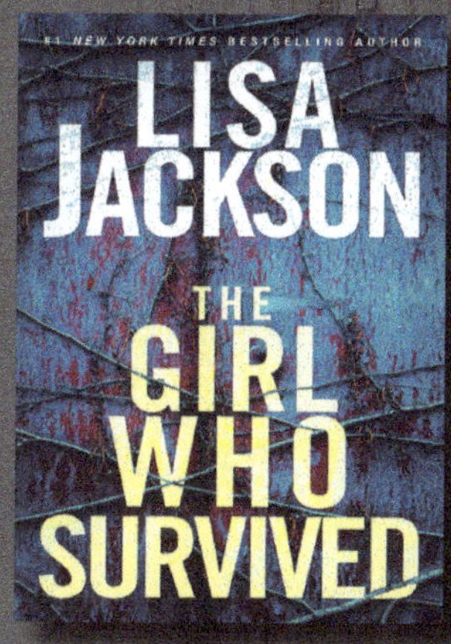

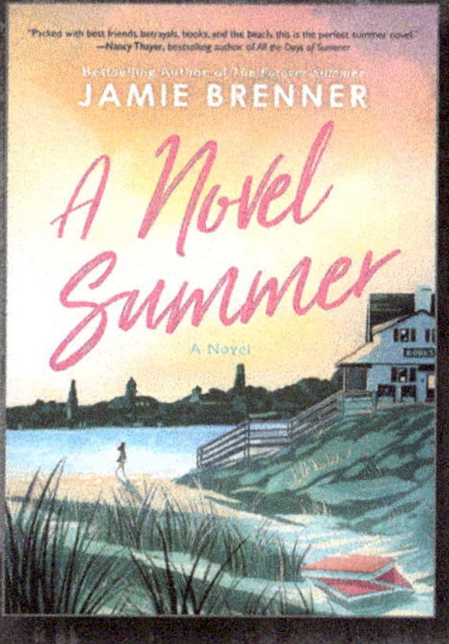

A Novel Summer
JAMIE BRENNER

"The perfect summer beach read! Rival bookshops, second chance romance, friend drama, it was the perfect book to curl up and escape to the Cape."
—Pamela Kelley, bestselling author of Bookshop by the Bay

https://amzn.to/3WtdCpF

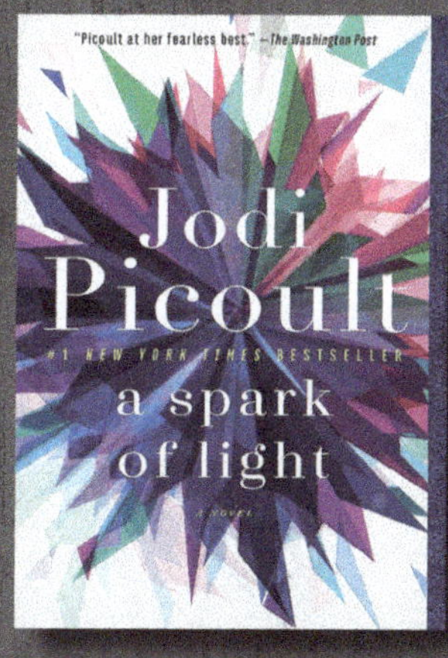

A Spark of Light
JODI PICOULT

"Picoult at her fearless best . . . Timely, balanced and certain to inspire debate."
—The Washington Post

https://amzn.to/3SzeesG

The Beekeeper of Aleppo
CHRISTY LEFTERI

"Beekeeper Nuri and his wife, Afra, are devastated by the Syrian civil war. After violence claims their child and Afra's eyesight, the couple is forced to flee Aleppo and make the fraught journey to Britain—and an uncertain future."
—USA Today

https://amzn.to/4dsnhnu

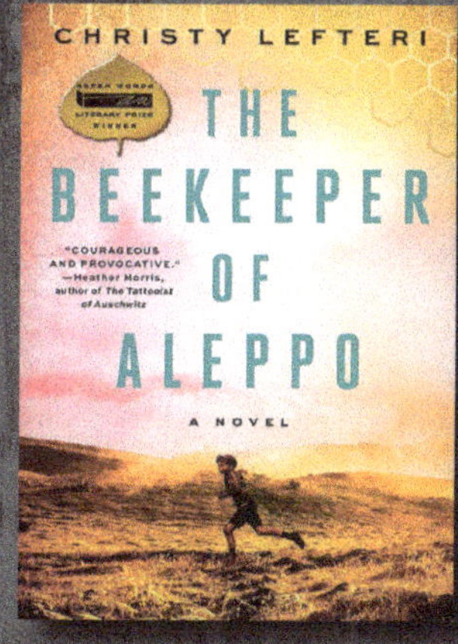

A Novel Love Story
ASHLEY POSTON

"Ashley Poston has written another clever, emotional love story part fantasy, part romcom—perfect for passing a day or three by the pool."
—Harper's Bazaar

https://amzn.to/3WKwcLt

CON**TENT**

**MEET THE AUTHORS
BEHIND THE HITS**

COVER

The Passion Behind History Matters and Its Impact on Berry's Writing
STEVE BERRY
Unveiling the Past

PUBLISHER: Novelist Post, A Subsidiary of Newyox Media. 200 Suite 134-146 Curtain Road, EC2A 3AR London
t: +44 79 3847 8420 editor@novelistpost.com II http://newyox.com
EDITORIAL: Ben F. Oncu, Editor-in-Chief, Ermesto Kara, Managing Editor, C. Rochelle, Art Editor, Delfina Reneta, Content Editor,
Reporters: Adelina Alban , Carine Leary, Amy Stanford, Z. Robers, Albert Cassandra CONTRIBUTOS: Claudine D. Reyes, Esma Arslan, Adrian T.
We assume no responsibility for unsolicited manuscripts or art materials provided from our contributors.

EDITOR'S LETTER

Welcome to the inaugural issue of Novelist Post, a magazine dedicated to celebrating the brilliance of bestselling, award-winning, and exceptional authors in the realms of novels, romance, and fiction. We are thrilled to introduce this new generation publication, which stands apart from conventional magazines by offering a unique and comprehensive platform for literary voices.

Novelist Post is available in print across 190 countries and through thousands of retailers and platforms, including Amazon, Barnes & Noble, Walmart, Waterstones, and many more. Additionally, our content is accessible online, electronically, and on social media, ensuring that you can engage with us wherever you are.

In this debut issue, we are honored to feature Steve Berry, a master of the historical thriller and a New York Times bestselling author, as our cover star. With twenty-three bestsellers to his name, including "The Atlas Maneuver," "The Last Kingdom," and "The Omega Factor," Berry has captivated readers worldwide with his meticulously researched and intricately plotted novels. His works, translated into 41 languages and sold in 52 countries, consistently dominate bestseller lists, a testament to his global appeal and storytelling prowess.

At the core of Berry's novels lies a deep passion for history, a passion he shares with his wife, Elizabeth. Together, they founded History Matters, a foundation dedicated to historic preservation. Through lectures, workshops, and fundraising events, they have raised over $1.5 million to save endangered historic treasures. This commitment to history is not just a backdrop for Berry's novels but a driving force that shapes his narratives and characters.

Berry's accolades are numerous, including the American Library Association's spokesperson for National Preservation Week, the Royden B. Davis Distinguished Author Award, and the Silver Bullet Award from International Thriller Writers. His dedication to both his craft and his philanthropic efforts has earned him a place among the most respected authors of our time.

In this exclusive interview with Novelist Post, Steve Berry delves into the intricacies of blending historical accuracy with contemporary thrillers, the inspiration behind his beloved protagonist Cotton Malone, and the collaborative process of co-writing with other authors. He also shares insights into his rigorous research methods and the challenges of resonating with a global audience. Join us as we explore the mind of a literary giant whose work continues to enthrall and educate readers around the world.

In addition to our feature on Steve Berry, our editorial team has curated a selection of profiles on award-winning and exceptional authors, including Shane Svorec, William G. Duffy, Cordell Parvin, Tricia Copeland, Jack Erickson, Penny C. Knight, Joseph Fagarazzi, Mimi Barbour, Robert Emmers, Christina McDonald, Janice Angelique, S. M. Stevens, D.M. Foley, Victoria Chatham, Tessa Barrie, Karen Nappa, Chrysteen Braun, G. S. Gerry, Toni Anderson, Kirsten Pursell, Jason Gabriel, J.T. Ellison, Katherine H. Klemp, Wendy Zuccarello, and L. M. Montes. Each of these authors brings a unique voice and perspective to the literary world, and we are excited to share their stories with you.

If you are a fiction author and would like to be featured in Novelist Post, please contact us for interview opportunities. We are always on the lookout for new and compelling voices to showcase in our magazine.

Thank you for joining us on this exciting journey. We hope you enjoy reading Novelist Post as much as we have enjoyed creating it.

Ben F. Oncu

Editor-in-Chief

Finding Purpose Through Pain

Shane Svorec uses her unique experiences and heartfelt storytelling to foster empathy, understanding, and connection, inspiring readers to appreciate life's simple joys.

BY DAN PETERS

How Shane Svorec Uses Words to Foster Empathy and Connection

Shane Svorec, a lifelong writer and advocate, has dedicated her career to crafting heartfelt narratives that resonate with readers of all ages. Her unique ability to string words together in a way that evokes deep emotions and fosters genuine connections has earned her acclaim and admiration. Svorec's writing is not just about telling stories; it's about creating a space for empathy, understanding, and reflection. Her works aim to rekindle the joy of appreciating life's simple pleasures and inspire readers to recognize the impact they can have on the world and each other.

Growing up in a transient lifestyle, moving across the country and living in various places, significantly shaped Svorec's worldview. This upbringing instilled in her a belief that every experience and encounter offers valuable lessons and opportunities to connect with others. Her book, "Broken Little Believer: Finding Purpose in All the Pretty Painful Pieces," exemplifies this perspective. Through her personal journey of finding purpose in pain, she illustrates how hardship can be a catalyst for growth and understanding. This memoir is not only a testament to her resilience but also a beacon of hope for others navigating their own struggles.

Svorec's experiences with the foster care system as both a child and as a foster parent deeply inform her advocacy work and storytelling. Her intimate understanding of the foster care system's gaps and limitations drives her to support and uplift those in need. By sharing her firsthand knowledge and wisdom, she emphasizes the importance of resilience and empathy. Her advocacy is rooted in the belief that one's past does not dictate their future and that everyone has the potential to rise above their circumstances and make a positive impact.

Her children's book, *The Busy Bridge That Got Its Break*, uses the Tappan Zee Bridge as a metaphor to convey important life lessons. Inspired by her childhood memories and adult reflections, Svorec personifies the bridge to tell a story of unnoticed strength and endurance.

This heartwarming tale encourages readers to slow down and appreciate the often overlooked people and structures around them. It serves as a reminder of the importance of recognizing and valuing the unnoticed contributions in our lives.

Svorec describes herself as having the heart of a hippie and the faith of a missionary. This duality is evident in her writing, where her free-spirited appreciation for nature and everyday beauty intersects with a deep, purposeful commitment to making a difference. Her approach to life—celebrating small moments and practicing gratitude—inspires others to do the same, prompting them to slow down and savor the simple gifts around them.

As an active community member involved in mental health and crisis intervention, Svorec's real-world experiences deeply influence the themes and characters in her books. Her dedication to supporting the underdog and giving a voice to the misunderstood is a driving force behind her writing. By transforming personal and vulnerable experiences into powerful narratives, she encourages readers to embrace their own stories and find strength in their authenticity.

Shane Svorec's upcoming third book, set for release this fall, is highly anticipated by her readers. Through her expressive writing and commitment to advocacy, she continues to touch hearts, provoke thought, and inspire change. Her work is a testament to the power of storytelling in fostering empathy and understanding in an often disconnected world.

Shane Svorec's writing captures genuine emotions and inspires readers to live authentically and appreciate the beauty around them.

> *As a little girl, whenever something bad happened, I would tell myself there had to be a reason or purpose. I would have crumbled without this habitual internal dialogue and my reliance on faith. We don't survive tragedies if we don't have hope for the future. Without much support, I knew I had to be strong and push myself to keep going."*

Shane Svorec

Unveiling the Hidden Gospel

William G. Duffy explores the Gospel of Thomas, revealing profound spiritual truths beyond conventional beliefs, inviting introspection and transformation.

BY BEN ALAN

William G. Duffy's Spiritual Journey Through Thomas

William G. Duffy, an esteemed figure in the realm of spiritual exploration, has meticulously crafted a profound analysis of the Gospel of Thomas in his latest work, "Hidden Gospel of Thomas," published by SilverWood Books Ltd. Delving into this ancient text with the precision of a scholar and the insight of a seasoned spiritual seeker, Duffy's exploration transcends traditional scholarly boundaries.

Born in Washington, DC, and shaped by his academic pursuits at Syracuse University and the University of Toronto, Duffy's journey into the Gospel of Thomas began over three decades ago. His fascination with this enigmatic manuscript stemmed from a deep-seated curiosity about fundamental truths—questions that challenge the very nature of perception and existence.

The acclaim garnered by Duffy's book, including the prestigious 2021 IAN Book of the Year Award, reflects its groundbreaking nature. Rather than merely dissecting historical contexts or theological frameworks, Duffy uncovers layers of wisdom concealed within the gospel's cryptic verses. His interpretation invites readers to embark on a transformative journey of introspection and spiritual awakening, echoing the gospel's invitation to uncover hidden truths within oneself.

In his interview with Reader's House magazine, Duffy elucidates the motivations driving his extensive research. His inclination to question entrenched beliefs and probe the essence of spirituality led him to the Gospel of Thomas, which he views not just as a historical artifact but as a timeless guide to understanding the "Kingdom of the Father"—a spiritual realm within, often obscured by egoic constructs.

Central to Duffy's interpretation is the gospel's non-dualistic philosophy, challenging conventional religious paradigms by emphasizing direct spiritual experience over dogma. He clarifies that despite its discovery among Gnostic texts, the Gospel of Thomas stands apart, devoid of the elaborate cosmologies and rituals typically associated with Gnosticism. Duffy's rigorous scholarship reframes this gospel, presenting it as a profound testament to universal truths accessible through personal revelation and introspection.

Looking ahead, Duffy remains committed to unraveling the gospel's complexities and implications. His ongoing work promises to reshape perceptions of Christianity and spirituality, inviting readers to explore profound truths that have the potential to revolutionize their understanding of faith and existence.

In a world rife with doctrinal rigidity, William G. Duffy's insights offer a refreshing perspective—a call to rediscover spirituality beyond the confines of tradition and orthodoxy. Through his book, he beckons readers to embrace the challenge of uncovering the hidden truths of the Gospel of Thomas, inviting them to embark on a journey of self-discovery and spiritual illumination.

For more on William G. Duffy's research and insights, visit his website at williamgduffy.com, where he continues to share his explorations of the Gospel of Thomas and its profound implications for contemporary spirituality.

William G. Duffy, acclaimed author and spiritual scholar, delves into the depths of ancient wisdom in his latest work.

The Gospel of Thomas is such a vast topic. If taken seriously, it could revolutionize Christianity. If truly understood, it has that power. How could I write about anything else? I will continue to write about this gospel, its implications, and insights."

William G. Duffy

TRANSFORMING LEGAL LIVES

Cordell Parvin's Journey from Construction Law to Empowering Lawyers through Coaching

Cordell Parvin transitioned from a successful construction lawyer to a renowned career coach, inspiring over a thousand lawyers with practical, holistic coaching focused on professional growth, personal fulfillment, and collaboration.

Cordell Parvin: From construction lawyer to celebrated career coach, inspiring a new generation of legal professionals.

In the often intense and demanding world of law, the transition from a courtroom advocate to a career coach might seem like an unconventional path. Yet, for Cordell Parvin, this shift has not only transformed his own career but also inspired and guided over a thousand lawyers across the United States and Canada. Parvin's journey from practicing construction law to becoming a renowned legal coach underscores the profound impact of mentorship and personal fulfillment in professional success.

A Legal Career Rooted in Excellence

Cordell Parvin's name has become synonymous with career development within the legal sector, particularly in client acquisition and professional growth for attorneys. With a distinguished career in construction law spanning over 38 years, Parvin has represented some of the top contractors in the country. However, it was his work in coaching new partners within his law firm that ignited a deeper passion.

In 2004, despite having his best year professionally, Parvin found greater fulfillment in helping young lawyers navigate their careers. This realization led him to leave his practice and dedicate himself entirely to coaching lawyers. His transition from a high-earning attorney to a full-time coach highlights a significant career shift driven by a desire to make a more meaningful contribution to the legal profession.

Practical Coaching Methodologies

Parvin's approach to coaching is both practical and holistic, focusing on goal setting, time management, and achieving a balance between professional obligations and personal life. His methodologies are informed by his extensive experience and his roles as a speaker, writer, and blogger on career and client development. Through his engaging presentations at law firms and bar associations, Parvin has established himself as a thought leader in the legal industry.

Since starting his coaching career in 2005, Parvin has worked with lawyers from diverse backgrounds, providing invaluable insights into the challenges they face. He advocates for a structured approach to professional growth, emphasizing the importance of investing time in both career development and personal well-being. This dual focus is essential for achieving long-term success and fulfillment in the legal profession.

Engaging Young Lawyers Through Storytelling

Parvin's books, such as "Say Ciao to Chow Mein: Conquering Career Burnout" and "Rising Star," utilize a storytelling approach inspired by Ken Blanchard's business parables. These narratives deliver serious career advice in a relatable and engaging manner, addressing issues like career burnout and the need for a balanced life. By sharing personal anecdotes and practical solutions, Parvin offers young lawyers a roadmap for navigating the complexities of their careers while maintaining their well-being.

Cultivating a Collaborative Culture

One of the key challenges in the legal profession is shifting from a competitive mindset to a collaborative one. Parvin emphasizes the importance of cultivating a collaborative culture within law firms, which can be achieved by hiring lawyers with strong interpersonal skills, rewarding teamwork, and prioritizing the development of junior lawyers. This approach not only enhances team dynamics but also fosters a more supportive and productive work environment.

Essential Advice for Aspiring Rainmakers

For young lawyers aspiring to become successful rainmakers, Parvin's most crucial piece of advice is to identify a compelling "why" behind their ambitions. This motivational cornerstone drives the creation of comprehensive plans, which span various timeframes and instill the commitment and discipline required to follow through. By maintaining a clear focus on their goals and understanding their underlying motivations, young lawyers can navigate their careers with greater purpose and determination.

Cordell Parvin's transition from practicing law to coaching has had a transformative impact on the careers of countless lawyers. His practical, storytelling approach to career development, combined with his emphasis on personal fulfillment and collaborative culture, offers invaluable guidance to young lawyers. Parvin's journey serves as an inspiring testament to the power of mentorship and the importance of pursuing a career that aligns with one's passions and values.

> *Cordell Parvin's insightful and transformative coaching has profoundly shaped the careers and lives of countless lawyers in North America.*

Discovering Magic in Every Story

Tricia Copeland discusses her diverse storytelling, personal influences, and the magic of resilience in her acclaimed works across various genres.

Tricia Copeland's storytelling is a masterful blend of resilience, imagination, and personal growth, inspiring readers across multiple genres.

BY DAN PETERS

Tricia Copeland believes in finding magic. She thinks magic infuses every aspect of our lives, whether it is the magic of falling in love, discovering a new passion, or a book that transports us to another world. Her most recent series, the Realm Chronicles epic fantasies, finds a fae princess fighting for her kingdom, people, and very own life, and includes a host of fantastical beings.

Copeland's books delve deeply into themes of resilience, personal growth, and the discovery of one's own strength. When asked what draws her to these themes, she explains, "Writing stories with characters that exemplify resilience, growth, and inner strength, what I call magic, is my passion. As an anorexia survivor, I know what it feels like to lose hope. But I've also experienced the overwhelming drive that comes from believing things can be better. I couldn't always see how

to make changes, but I watched mentors and found my path. I hope that reading my characters' stories can help others move through challenges and inspire them to find their own inner magic."

From contemporary romance to dystopian fiction to paranormal urban fantasy, Copeland's work spans various genres. Her inspiration for such diverse storytelling comes from her eclectic reading habits. "I love reading and my book lists span from non-fiction, to romance, historical fiction, dystopian, and fantasy. Mirroring my reading habits, my novels reflect these different interests. I'm inspired by stories of growth and resilience, so my plots tend to highlight characters that exemplify those traits," she shares. For instance, her Kingdom Journals series features a vampire-witch hybrid navigating acceptance and belonging in a world where witches and vampires blend into society unbeknownst to humans.

Copeland's Being Me Series

draws heavily from her personal experience, particularly in overcoming anorexia. This personal journey significantly influences her writing process. "The Being Me series became my first entry into the author and publishing world. With these books, I aim to give hope to those that struggle with eating disorders and mental illness. I chose to write about my experience as a fiction work, changing settings and details to protect the anonymity of those that shared in my journey. Even with fictionalizing the story, sharing that part of my life is a vulnerable and challenging endeavor. The connections I've made as a result have been an enriching trade-off," she reveals.

In her dystopian novels like *Lovelock Ones* and *Torch,* Copeland creates immersive worlds and compelling characters facing extraordinary challenges. She is drawn to the dystopian genre because it allows for escape and sparks imagination. "Much like fantasy, dystopian fiction transports us to different settings, enabling escape and sparking imagination. Many dystopian works push me to wonder how I would react in given scenarios. Would I be brave and strong enough to face harsh conditions and make tough choices?" she muses. Balancing world-building with character development is crucial in her storytelling. "World building in a dystopian novel can be a crucial element in creating some of the challenges characters will face. How characters react to the environment and situations they face over the course of the story allows opportunity for character development," she explains.

Copeland's Kingdom Journals Series, particularly *Kingdom of*

Embers, has garnered critical acclaim and awards. Her love for fantasy, especially vampire fantasy, inspired her to delve into the paranormal urban fantasy genre. "Even though I read in many genres, fantasy, in particular vampire fantasy, is my favorite. After publishing the Being Me series, I knew I wanted to write a vampire series. My aim became to create something new without veering too far from the expectations of the trope," she says. The series features Alena, a vampire-witch teen, and follows her quest to save the witch lines from eternal purgatory, blending supernatural elements seamlessly into the narrative.

As the founder of True Bird Publishing LLC, Copeland oversees the publication of her own books. Her experience as an independent author has shaped her approach to publishing. "I formed my publishing business to control the narrative for my books. Because each story and character is special to me, I didn't want them to be commandeered. I've had amazing editors and cover creators who help me refine and produce the best versions of my stories possible," she states. Her advice to aspiring authors considering self-publishing is to surround themselves with good people who support their journey, whether they choose indie publishing or working with a traditional publisher.

Tricia Copeland's journey as an author is a testament to the magic that can be found in resilience, personal growth, and diverse storytelling. Her works continue to inspire and transport readers to worlds where magic is real and inner strength triumphs.

Crafting Authentic Thrillers

Jack Erickson, acclaimed for his Milan Thriller Series, blends meticulous research and deep cultural insights to create gripping narratives centered around Italy's anti-terrorism police, DIGOS.

Novelist Jack Erickson Explores Milan's Dark Underbelly

Acclaimed author Jack Erickson has carved a niche for himself in the world of international thrillers, mysteries, and noir fiction. His Milan Thriller Series, which delves into the world of Italy's anti-terrorism police, DIGOS, has captivated readers with its authentic portrayal of Italian society and intricate plots. With titles like "Thirteen Days in Milan," "No One Sleeps," "Vesuvius Nights," and "The Lonely Assassin," Erickson's work is deeply rooted in the historical and cultural fabric of Milan.

Erickson's connection to Milan began serendipitously during a retirement trip in 2011. A visit to Stazione Centrale sparked the idea for what would become his first Milan thriller. "Thirteen Days in Milan" emerged from this lightning-bolt inspiration, with Erickson immersing himself in contemporary Italian literature and hiring a researcher to provide invaluable local insights. This rigorous approach to research has become a hallmark of his writing process.

The author's dedication to authenticity is evident in his annual trips to Italy, where he gathers information and inspiration. Erickson has established connections with high-level officials in Milan's DIGOS, enabling him to portray sophisticated surveillance and investigative procedures accurately. His deep engagement with Italian culture, including intensive language studies and frequent visits to Milanese landmarks like La Scala, enriches his narratives with a genuine sense of place.

Erickson's protagonist, Sylvia de Matteo, reflects his meticulous character development. As a successful single mother who faces kidnapping and intense trials, Sylvia's resilience is crafted through Erickson's detailed discussions with his Milanese researchers and friends. Their real-life experiences and stories infuse Sylvia's character with authenticity, making her struggles and triumphs resonate deeply with readers.

Balancing the rich tapestry of Italian society and culture with the pacing and suspense of a thriller is no small feat, yet Erickson manages this seamlessly. Historical events, such as the 1978 kidnapping and assassination of Prime Minister Aldo Moro by the Brigate Rosse, are woven into the fabric of his stories, providing a backdrop that enhances the narrative's depth and urgency. This blending of history with contemporary issues allows readers to immerse themselves fully in the complex world of Milan's political and social landscape.

Comparisons to renowned authors like Donna Leon and Andrea Camilleri are both flattering and indicative of Erickson's impact on the genre. He draws inspiration from these literary giants but brings his unique voice and perspective to the table. Erickson's thrillers, set in the dynamic and historic city of Milan, stand out for their rich detail and compelling storytelling.

Erickson's background as an Air Force intelligence officer and a U.S. Senate speechwriter has significantly influenced his writing. The skills honed in these roles—research, interviewing, and precise, impactful writing—translate seamlessly into his novels. His ability to craft intricate narratives and engaging dialogue stems from decades of experience in fields that demand clarity and persuasiveness.

Jack Erickson's journey from crafting speeches and non-fiction to creating thrilling fiction has been marked by a relentless pursuit of authenticity and a deep love for Italy. His Milan Thriller Series not only entertains but also offers a window into the complexities of Italian society, all while keeping readers on the edge of their seats. With each new book, Erickson continues to solidify his reputation as a master of international thrillers.

Erickson masterfully combines rich historical context with thrilling plots, earning him a revered place among international thriller writers.

My careers as an Air Force Intelligence Officer and later a speechwriter for three American Senators taught me how to research, interview important people, and reporting / writing a document that would be read by many. . I have been a writer for more than 50 years and had two careers in publishing, writing five books on the early days of microbreweries and later writing international thrillers, short mysteries, true crime."

Jack Erickson

Unveiling Resilience Through Life's Trials

Penny Christian Knight shares her journey of resilience, healing, and growth, detailing her experiences of trauma and recovery in her autobiographical memoir trilogy to inspire and guide others.

A Journey from Trauma to Triumph

Penny Christian Knight's life is a vivid illustration of the resilience inherent in the human spirit. Throughout her diverse career, which has included modeling, acting, and various office roles, Penny found her true calling as a social psychotherapist. Her midlife return to academia at the age of 45, where she pursued degrees in psychology and English, marked a significant turning point, allowing her to embrace her passions fully.

At 89, Penny retired from her private practice and shifted her focus to completing her autobiographical memoir trilogy. The first installment, "DEVELOPING RESILIENCE: Secrets, Sex Abuse, and the Quest for Love and Inner Peace," delves deeply into her personal experiences, exploring themes of trauma, healing, and resilience. In an exclusive interview with Reader's House Magazine, Penny shared the motivations behind her decision to reveal such intimate details of her life.

Reflecting on the emotional challenges she faced while revisiting traumatic memories, Penny explained, "As I developed resilience, I found it helped me face many challenges that confronted me. Early on, I learned how to repress unpleasant memories... But it is essential to get in touch with our feelings, to name and express them to a trustworthy and safe person."

Penny's journey toward resilience has profoundly shaped her perspective on life. She emphasizes the critical role of resilience in overcoming adversity and finding hope. "I hope readers will learn that they can survive almost anything and that it helps to develop friendships with compassionate friends," she explains. "We must find and develop ourselves to become whatever we are meant to be and not run and hide."

Her memoir is not only a testament to her personal resilience but also a beacon of hope for readers grappling with their own challenges. Through candid storytelling and unwavering honesty, Penny Christian Knight inspires others to find the courage and strength to overcome their struggles.

The motivation to share her deeply personal story came after an authentic personal essay she wrote during a workshop at the Omega Institute of Holistic Studies. Realizing the therapeutic power of writing, Penny decided to embark on her memoir journey at 80. She felt a mission to share her story to help others find hope and courage. The safety of having many named individuals in her story already passed allowed her to open up fully.

Navigating the emotional challenges of revisiting her past was a complex process, but one that Penny was prepared for. By the time she began writing her memoirs, she had already processed much of her trauma through counseling and her own work as a psychotherapist. "Having become a psychotherapist myself also helped me process the traumas before the creation of the books," she notes.

Resilience, a recurring theme in her life, is central to Penny's narrative. She recounts learning to repress unpleasant memories to survive and later, the importance of engaging in activities that kept her safe and connected to others. These coping mechanisms helped her develop wisdom and understanding over time. "It is essential to get in touch with our feelings, to name and express them to a trustworthy and safe person," she emphasizes.

Through her memoir, Penny hopes to impart several key lessons to her readers. She advocates for the power of friendship, personal development, and the importance of not hiding from one's past. Writing, she found, was a powerful therapeutic tool. "We can write to the person who harmed us and tell them off but not send the letter. This is highly therapeutic," she advises.

Penny's experiences as a social psychotherapist significantly influenced the narrative and themes of her memoir. Her professional background provided her with unique insights and a deeper understanding of trauma and healing. This expertise enriched her commentary and reflections throughout her books, offering valuable guidance to readers with similar backgrounds.

One of the most cathartic and healing moments for Penny during the writing process was revisiting the section on her marriage and divorce. Editing and rereading that material allowed her to access and process emotions she hadn't fully experienced at the time, providing a sense of closure and understanding.

Penny Christian Knight's memoir is a powerful testament to the resilience of the human spirit. Through her candid narrative, she not only chronicles her own journey of healing but also offers a source of inspiration and guidance for others facing their own struggles. Her story is a compelling reminder that, even in our darkest moments, there is always hope for growth and transformation.

Penny C. Knight's courageous storytelling and profound insights make her memoir an invaluable beacon of hope and resilience.

> *I hope readers will learn that they can survive almost anything and that it helps to develop friendships with compassionate friends. We survivors go on despite what happens to us. We must find and develop ourselves to become whatever we are meant to be and not run and hide."*

Penny Christian Knight

STEVE BERRY

Unveiling the Past

<u>The Amber Room</u> is a thrilling adventure that masterfully blends history, intrigue, and suspense. Following Atlanta judge Rachel Cutler and her ex-husband Paul, the novel takes readers on a gripping treasure hunt across Germany. With shadowy characters and ruthless killers, it's a captivating debut in international thrillers.

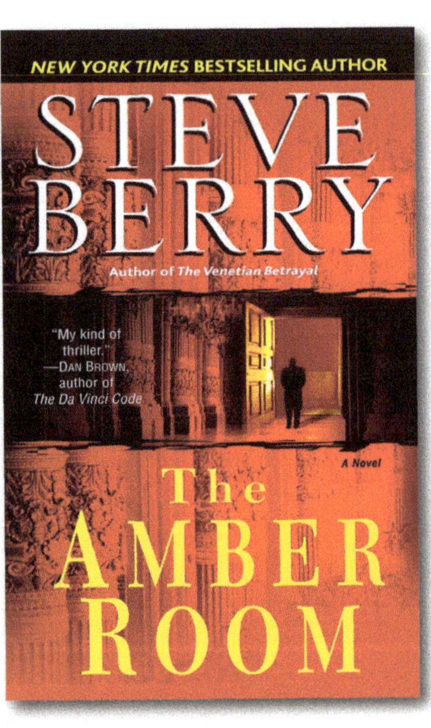

BY CHIARA ROCCIA

Steve Berry discusses his passion for history, the creation of Cotton Malone, his collaborative writing process, and the meticulous research behind his globally acclaimed historical thrillers.

Steve Berry, a master of the historical thriller, has captivated readers worldwide with his meticulously researched and intricately plotted novels. With twenty-three bestsellers to his name, including The Atlas Maneuver, The Last Kingdom, and The Omega Factor, Berry has established himself as a titan in the literary world. His works, translated into 41 languages and sold in 52 countries, consistently dominate bestseller lists, a testament to his global appeal and storytelling prowess.

At the core of Berry's novels lies a deep passion for history, a passion he shares with his wife, Elizabeth. Together, they founded History Matters, a foundation dedicated to historic preservation. Through lectures, workshops, and fundraising events, they have raised over $1.5 million to save endangered historic treasures. This commitment to history is not just a backdrop for Berry's novels but a driving force that shapes his narratives and characters.

Berry's accolades are numerous, including the American Library Association's spokesperson for National Preservation Week, the Royden B. Davis Distinguished Author Award, and the Silver Bullet Award from International Thriller Writers. His dedication to both his craft and his philanthropic efforts has earned him a place among the most respected authors of our time.

In this exclusive interview with Novelist Post Magazine, Steve Berry delves into the intricacies of blending historical accuracy with contemporary thrillers, the inspiration behind his beloved protagonist Cotton Malone, and the collaborative process of co-writing with other authors. He also shares insights into his rigorous research methods and the challenges of resonating with a global audience. Join us as we explore the mind of a literary giant whose work continues to enthrall and educate readers around the world.

Continued *on page 10*

Steve Berry, the New York Times Bestselling author of twenty-four novels, shares his passion for history and storytelling.

Your novels often blend historical mysteries with contemporary thrillers. What draws you to this genre, and how do you balance historical accuracy with the demands of crafting a suspenseful narrative?

I love stories with action, history, secrets and conspiracies. So, naturally, when I began to write I wrote those. I adhere to the philosophy to never write what you know. Instead, write what you love. I am also particularly intrigued with obscure details from the past. Things you don't know, but want to know more about. Especially those that have little to no explanation. Those are the best, since I can fashion whatever explanation works for the story. My niche, though, is to keep my novels about 90% accurate to history. The closer the better. For that 10% I change there is a writer's note in the back of all the books that explains where and why that happened.

History Matters is a foundation you co-founded with your wife, Elizabeth, dedicated to historic preservation. How has your work with this foundation influenced your writing, particularly in novels like The Templar Legacy and The Malta Exchange?

It's really the other way around. The writing not only gave birth to History Matters, it also influenced its development. In school, history can seem the most tedious of subjects. So many facts, figures and dates that mean little to nothing. But history is not something obscure or unimportant. It's a story — the story of us. Which plays a vital role in our everyday lives. We study our past in order to achieve greater influence over our future. It is from history that we learn what to champion and what to avoid. Decision-making around the world, every day, is based on what came before us. Why? Because history matters.

You've co-written novels with both Grant Blackwood and novellas with M.J. Rose. How does the collaborative writing process differ from writing solo, and what unique challenges or advantages do you find in each approach?

One's a team, the other is a solo endeavor. And, once on a team, everyone has to be a team player. I've been lucky. Both of my collaborations have worked great. In each I develop the initial story idea and a rough outline of the plot. Then Grant and MJ take that and write a first draft of the entire work. They have total freedom to go wherever and do whatever is needed for the story. Once they are done I take the manuscript and re-write it, placing it in my voice and making sure the world we created and the characters are consistent with previous books. When we're done with have a novel or a novella. It's a true collaborative effort.

Your protagonist, Cotton Malone, has become a beloved figure in the thriller genre. How has Cotton evolved over the course of the series, and what aspects of his character do you find most challenging or rewarding to develop?

Cotton was born in Copenhagen while I was sitting at a café in Højbro Plads, a popular Danish square. That's why Cotton owns a bookshop there. I wanted a character with government ties and a background that would make him, if threatened, formidable. But I also wanted him to be

human, with flaws. Since I love rare books, it was natural that Cotton would too, so he became a Justice Department operative, turned bookseller, who manages, from time to time, to find trouble. I also gave him an eidetic memory, since, well, who wouldn't like one of those? At the same time, Cotton is clearly a man in conflict. His marriage has failed, he maintains a difficult relationship with his teenage son, and he's lousy with women. When I created him in The Templar Legacy (2006) I never conceived that he'd be around 21 years and 19 books later. But over the course of those books he's definitely changed. Evolved. Become more introspective. Not afraid to show emotion. He's definitely matured.

The Omega Factor and The Museum of Mysteries explore intricate conspiracies and ancient artifacts. What inspired these particular storylines, and how do you research and weave together historical artifacts and mysteries into your plots?

For The Omega Factor it was visiting Belgium and seeing the Ghent Altarpiece. What an incredible work of art. The Museum of Mysteries was born after a trip to the village of Eze in France. What a spectacular place. To incorporate locales and artifacts like those takes time.

STEVE BERRY

Steve Berry is the New York Times and #1 internationally bestselling author of twenty-four novels, which include: The Medici Return, The Atlas Maneuver, The Last Kingdom, The Omega Factor, The Kaiser's Web, The Warsaw Protocol, The Malta Exchange, The Bishop's Pawn, The Lost Order, The 14th Colony, The Patriot Threat, The Lincoln Myth, The King's Deception, The Columbus Affair, The Jefferson Key, The Emperor's Tomb, The Paris Vendetta, The Charlemagne Pursuit, The Venetian Betrayal, The Alexandria Link, The Templar Legacy, The Third Secret, The Romanov Prophecy, and The Amber Room. Steve has also co-written two novels with Grant Blackwood, Red Star Falling, and The 9th Man, both Luke Daniels Adventures, and four novellas with M. J. Rose: The End of Forever, The House of Long Ago, The Lake of Learning, and The Museum of Mysteries, all Cassiopeia Vitt tales. His books have been translated into 41 languages with over 26,000,000 copies in 52 countries. They consistently appear in the top echelon of The New York Times, USA Today, and Indie bestseller lists. Somewhere in the world, every thirty seconds, one of his novels is sold.

History lies at the heart of every Steve Berry novel. It's his passion, one he shares with his wife, Elizabeth, which led them to create History Matters, a foundation dedicated to historic preservation. Since 2009 Steve and Elizabeth have crossed the country to save endangered historic treasures, raising money via lectures, receptions, galas, luncheons, dinners, and their popular writers' workshops. To date, 3,500 students have attended those workshops with over $1.5 million dollars raised.

Steve's devotion to historic preservation was recognized by the American Library Association, which named Steve its spokesperson for National Preservation Week. Among his other honors are the Royden B. Davis Distinguished Author Award; the Barnes & Noble Writers for Writers Award given by Poets & Writers; the Anne Frank Human Writes Award; and the Silver Bullet, bestowed by International Thriller Writers for his philanthropic work. He has been chosen both the Florida and Georgia Writer of the Year. He's also an emeritus member of the Smithsonian Libraries Advisory Board. In 2010, a NPR survey named The Templar Legacy one of the top 100 thrillers ever written.

Steve was born and raised in Georgia, graduating from the Walter F. George School of Law at Mercer University. He was a trial lawyer for 30 years and held elective office for 14 of those years. He is a founding member of International Thriller Writers—a group of nearly 6,000 thriller writers from around the world—and served three years as its co-president.

For me it's an eighteen month process from start to finish. It begins six months before the writing starts, while I'm working on the book before. I do the preliminary research, sketching out the overall plot, gathering some of the 300 to 400 books that will eventually be used as sources, and outlining the first 100 pages. Once I finish the novel I'm working on and turn it in, I immediately start the new one. No break. No rest. Just right in. Then there is another twelve months of research and writing.

Your books have been translated into numerous languages and are widely read globally. How do you navigate cultural differences and ensure your stories resonate with an international audience while staying true to the historical contexts you explore?

I spend a good deal of time making sure that I get the details of the particular physical locales correct. Part of the appeal of my novels is that the locations become 'characters.' They are part of the story. Not just backdrops, but essential to the plot. And part of trying to get it right always involves at least one trip to the locales to see and feel firsthand what's there.

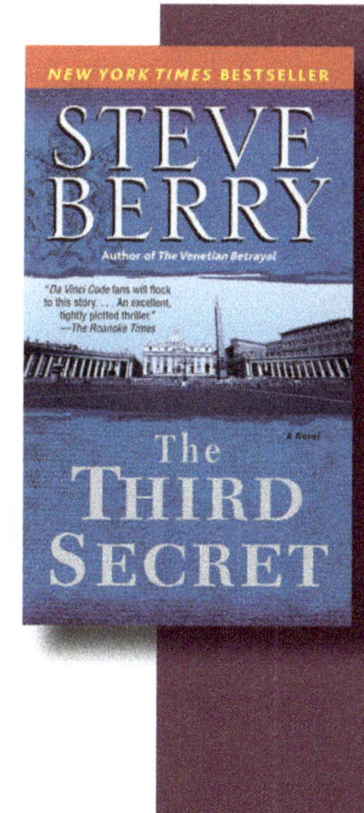

The *Third Secret* by Steve Berry is an electrifying international thriller that masterfully intertwines historical intrigue with contemporary suspense. Berry delves into one of the most enigmatic and controversial episodes in the history of the Catholic Church—the secrets of Fatima. The novel's gripping narrative takes readers from the serene landscapes of Fatima, Portugal, to the shadowy corridors of the Vatican, and beyond.

The story centers on Father Colin Michener, the papal secretary, who becomes increasingly alarmed by Pope Clement XV's obsessive visits to the Vatican's Riserva, a repository of the Church's most guarded documents. The Pope's distress is linked to the third secret of Fatima, a revelation that has long been shrouded in mystery and speculation. As Michener embarks on a perilous quest across Europe to uncover the truth, he encounters a web of murder, deceit, and forbidden love.

Berry's meticulous research and vivid storytelling bring to life the complex dynamics within the Vatican, the political machinations of ambitious cardinals, and the profound spiritual questions that the secrets of Fatima evoke. The novel's fast-paced plot and unexpected twists keep readers on the edge of their seats, while its exploration of faith, power, and truth resonates deeply.

The Third Secret is a compelling read that challenges the boundaries between history and fiction, leaving readers pondering the true nature of the Church's hidden truths. Berry's ability to blend historical facts with imaginative fiction makes this book a standout in the genre of religious thrillers.

Struggle to Success

JOSEPH FAGARAZZI

Joseph Fagarazzi's journey from an unwanted child in Venice to a successful author and businessman in Australia is a testament to resilience and determination. Born on September 7, 1951, his early years were marked by neglect and ridicule from biased parents, leading to a turbulent childhood. At a young age, he was placed in a convent as his parents immigrated to London. In 1960, thanks to his uncle's intervention, Joseph was reunited with his parents in England, only to face a cruel, passive-aggressive father. Despite these challenges, Joseph maintained an optimistic outlook, believing that hardship can drive one to survive and thrive.

Joseph Fagarazzi's resilience and determination shine through, making his story a powerful beacon of hope and inspiration.

In 1977, Joseph married his Australian wife at the Paddington registry office. A year later, they immigrated to Australia with just enough money for the flight. There, Joseph managed various clothing stores, eventually opening his own business in 1985. Over the next 22 years, he expanded to three stores and ventured into property development, successfully selling units and retaining some as rentals. In 2006, he sold his clothing business and pursued a career in real estate, obtaining a Diploma of Property Services and a Certificate IV in Property Services.

Retirement in 2015 allowed Joseph to rediscover his passion for art and to write a book, Escaping My Demons, which explores the deep emotional and physical hardships of his childhood. Writing began as a self-healing process with a five-page letter to himself, frozen as a symbolic act of halting his pain. This evolved into his memoir, bringing him peace and a realization that dwelling on the past hinders happiness. Through his writing, Joseph aims to help others facing similar challenges, urging them to look ahead and find what makes them happy.

Joseph's resilience was rooted in his self-belief, a challenging feat given his parents' negative perception of him. By changing his mindset and treating his life as a blueprint, he managed to overcome his demons and achieve success. He emphasizes that nothing changes unless one takes proactive steps to alter their circumstances. His advice to those in similar situations is to foster self-belief and understand that success is possible with determination and a positive outlook.

Key turning points in Joseph's life included his decision to fight for what he wanted without seeking handouts, thus retaining his dignity. He learned to carry his burdens alone, realizing that only he could resolve his internal struggles. His creative pursuits, particularly writing and painting, provided a therapeutic outlet, allowing him to process his past and find happiness.

Escaping My Demons conveys several important messages. Joseph hopes to inspire others who have faced childhood trauma, encouraging them to stop making excuses and change their mindsets. He also aims to reach parents who may be biased against their children, urging them to show love and support to all their offspring. His story is a powerful reminder that overcoming adversity is possible with persistence and a positive attitude.

Throughout his varied career in clothing retail, property development, and real estate, Joseph learned valuable lessons about perseverance and empathy. He attributes his success to the support of his loving wife and his determination to keep his inner fire burning. He advises aspiring entrepreneurs to follow their dreams, respect others, and cherish their achievements. Joseph's journey, encapsulated in his book, serves as a survival guide, illustrating that happiness and success are attainable despite the harshest beginnings.

Inspiration from Vancouver Island's Beauty

Mimi Barbour shares insights on her inspirations, writing process, and upcoming projects, revealing her commitment to creating captivating, humorous, and heartfelt romantic suspense stories that resonate deeply with readers.

BY DAN PETERS

Mimi Barbour, celebrated author of over 70 titles, Crafts Romance and Adventure

Renowned for her captivating narratives and an unmistakable flair for romance, NY Times bestselling author Mimi Barbour stands as a literary luminary among today's prolific authors. With a vast repertoire of over 70 titles, including nine series and numerous standalone works, Barbour's literary universe is as expansive as it is engaging.

Residing on the picturesque east coast of Vancouver Island, Barbour finds inspiration in the tranquil beauty of her surroundings, accompanied by her faithful canine companion and the loving embrace of family nearby. Yet, within this serene setting, a whirlwind of creativity swirls, fueled by Barbour's irrepressible passion for storytelling.

With a mischievous twinkle in her eye and a penchant for infusing her romances with humor, Barbour's writing captivates readers by transporting them from the mundanity of everyday life into realms of imagination. Her ultimate goal is to ensnare the hearts and minds of book lovers, whisking them away on fantastical journeys where the line between reality and fiction blurs effortlessly.

Barbour's literary influences are a testament to her wide-ranging tastes. She admires contemporary authors like Kristan Hannah and Nora Roberts, whose suspenseful works have left a significant mark on her. Her appreciation extends to biographies, having enjoyed the writings of Trevor Noah and Rachel Maddow, and she is keenly anticipating Liz Cheney's new book, drawn by Cheney's principled stand in the face of adversity.

Romantic suspense holds a special place in Barbour's heart, both as a reader and a writer. However, she doesn't shy away from exploring other genres, including contemporary romance and even paranormal tales. Her creative process is deeply influenced by current events, with news stories about school shootings, drug trafficking, and domestic terrorism often sparking the initial idea for a plot. This keen eye for contemporary issues ensures that her stories are not only engaging but also resonate with real-world relevance.

The characters in Barbour's stories often reflect real people from her life. Special Agent Murphy, for instance, is modeled after her late husband, whose complex personality and strong moral compass provided rich material for character development. This personal touch adds depth and authenticity to her narratives, making her characters relatable and memorable.

Barbour's writing routine is disciplined, inspired by the no-nonsense advice of literary icon Nora Roberts. She begins her day with a walk with her dog, followed by several hours of dedicated writing. This rigorous schedule reflects her belief that writing is a job that requires commitment and perseverance, regardless of whether the muse is present or not.

Her upcoming trilogy promises to be a thrilling addition to her oeuvre. Centered around Demi Fedora, a woman seeking solace amidst chaos, and the enigmatic Special Agent Lucifer, the trilogy is set to be a contemporary romance filled with action and suspense. Barbour's vivid imagination brings to life a derelict cabin in the forest, a wolf pup companion, and a rich gold prospector, weaving a narrative that promises continuous action and emotional depth.

As she continues to work on her next Special Agent story, inspired by themes of childhood bullying and complex heroism, it's clear that Barbour's dedication to her craft and her readers is unwavering. Her commitment to creating compelling, action-packed stories with well-developed characters ensures that her indelible mark on the world of literature will endure, captivating hearts and minds with each turn of the page.

Mimi Barbour masterfully blends romance, humor, and suspense, captivating readers with her authentic characters and engaging imaginative narratives.

> *As soon as I'm up and dressed, I start each day by taking my little dog for a walk. Once back home, I get my tea and go into my bedroom, slouch on my bed with my laptop and write at least 2- 5k words."*

Mimi Barbour

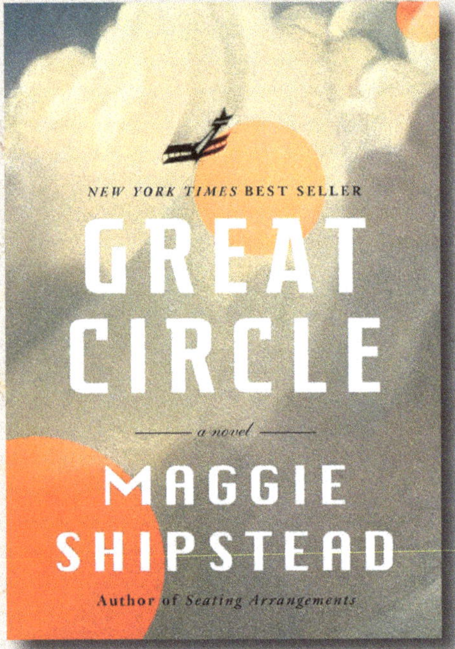

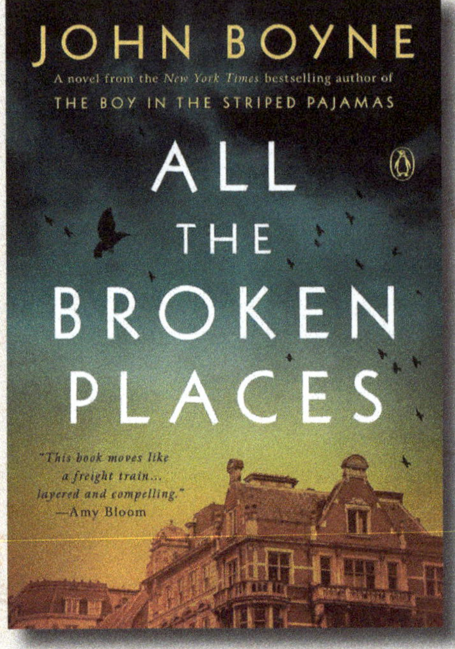

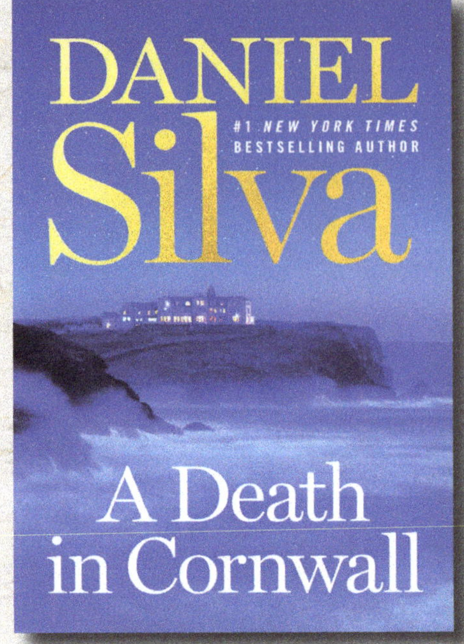

GREAT CIRCLE
by Maggie Shipstead

ALL THE BROKEN PLACES
by John Boyne

A DEATH IN CORNWALL
by Daniel Silva

"Great Circle" is a masterful, inspiring tale of adventure and identity, beautifully written with unforgettable characters and vivid storytelling.

Maggie Shipstead's *Great Circle* is a breathtaking literary achievement that intertwines the lives of two women separated by nearly a century but connected by their unyielding spirit and quest for freedom. This novel showcases Shipstead's prowess as a storyteller, weaving historical and contemporary narratives that captivate and inspire.

The story follows Marian Graves, an intrepid aviator whose life is marked by daring adventures and a relentless pursuit of the skies. From her early days flying in Alaska to her mysterious disappearance while attempting a great circle flight around the globe, Marian's journey is one of courage and resilience. Shipstead's meticulous research and vivid descriptions bring Marian's world to life, making her a character who feels both larger-than-life and deeply human.

Parallel to Marian's story is that of Hadley Baxter, a modern-day actress cast to play Marian in a biopic. Hadley's struggles with fame, identity, and personal demons provide a compelling counterpoint to Marian's narrative. As Hadley delves deeper into Marian's life, she embarks on her own journey of self-discovery. Shipstead skillfully navigates these dual timelines, creating a seamless and engaging narrative.

One of the novel's greatest strengths is its exploration of themes such as freedom, identity, and societal constraints. Marian's defiance of gender norms and her determination to carve out her own path in a male-dominated field are both inspiring and thought-provoking. Similarly, Hadley's struggle to reconcile her public persona with her true self resonates deeply.

Shipstead's prose is both lyrical and precise, capturing the grandeur of the skies and the intimate moments of her characters' lives. "Great Circle" is a profound exploration of living authentically and pursuing one's passions against all odds. This novel will linger in your thoughts long after you've turned the final page.

A poignant, beautifully written exploration of guilt, redemption, and history's shadows. Boyne's storytelling is both compelling and deeply moving.

John Boyne's *All the Broken Places* is a masterful exploration of guilt, redemption, and the long shadows cast by history. This poignant novel follows the life of Gretel Fernsby, a 91-year-old woman living in London, who harbors a dark secret from her past. As the story unfolds, Boyne skillfully weaves together past and present, revealing the haunting memories of Gretel's childhood in Nazi Germany and her struggle to reconcile with her family's legacy.

Boyne's narrative is both compelling and heart-wrenching, drawing readers into Gretel's internal conflict and the moral complexities she faces. The character development is exceptional, with Gretel portrayed as a deeply flawed yet sympathetic figure. Her interactions with her neighbors and the arrival of a new family in her building serve as catalysts for her to confront her past, leading to moments of profound introspection and emotional revelation.

The novel's pacing is well-balanced, with Boyne maintaining a delicate tension throughout. His prose is elegant and evocative, capturing the nuances of human emotion and the weight of historical trauma. The themes of forgiveness and the possibility of redemption are explored with sensitivity and depth, making *"All the Broken Places"* a thought-provoking read.

One of the novel's strengths is its ability to humanize its characters, presenting them in shades of gray rather than black and white. This nuanced portrayal encourages readers to reflect on the complexities of morality and the impact of history on individual lives.

All the Broken Places is a beautifully written and emotionally resonant novel that will stay with readers long after they turn the final page. John Boyne has crafted a powerful story that speaks to the enduring human capacity for change and forgiveness.

A masterful thriller, "A Death in Cornwall" captivate with its intricate plot, vivid settings, and compellin characters. An absolute must-read

Daniel Silva's latest novel, *A Death in Cornwall*, is a masterful blend of suspense, intrigue, and rich character development that will captivate both long-time fans and new readers alike. Set against the picturesque yet brooding backdrop of Cornwall, Silva weaves a tal that is as atmospheric as it is thrilling.

The story follows Gabriel Allon, the legendary art restorer and spy, who is drawn into a complex web of deceit and murder. When a prominent art dealer is found dead under mysterious circumstances, Allon is reluctantly pulled from his quiet life in Venice to unravel the truth. What begins as a seemingly straightforward investigation quickly spirals into a labyrinth of secrets involving stolen masterpieces, international conspiracies, and a shadowy adversary from Allon's past.

Silva's writing is as sharp and evocative as ever. Hi meticulous attention to detail brings the Cornish landscape to life, making it almost a character in its own right. The plot is tightly woven, with twists and turns that keep the reader guessing until the very end. Silva ability to blend historical facts with fiction adds a laye of depth and authenticity to the narrative, making the stakes feel incredibly real.

The character of Gabriel Allon continues to evolve, showing new facets of his personality and skills. His interactions with a cast of well-drawn supporting characters, including his wife Chiara and a host of new and familiar faces, add emotional weight and complexity to the story.

A Death in Cornwall is a testament to Daniel Silva' prowess as a storyteller. It's a gripping, intelligent thriller that not only entertains but also provokes though about the art world and the murky waters of internatio nal espionage. Whether you're a die-hard Silva fan or newcomer to his work, this novel is a must-read.

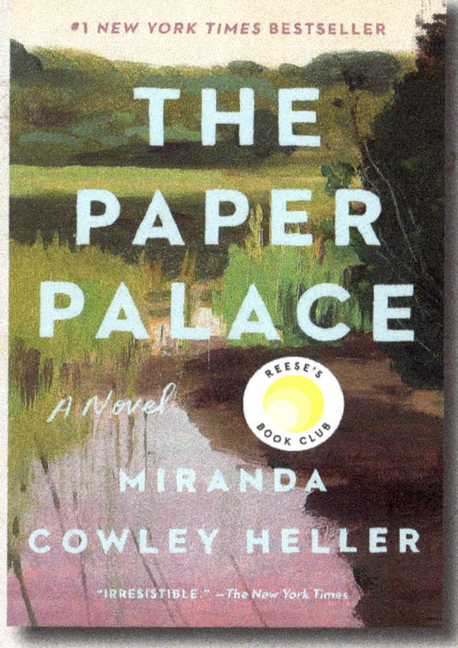

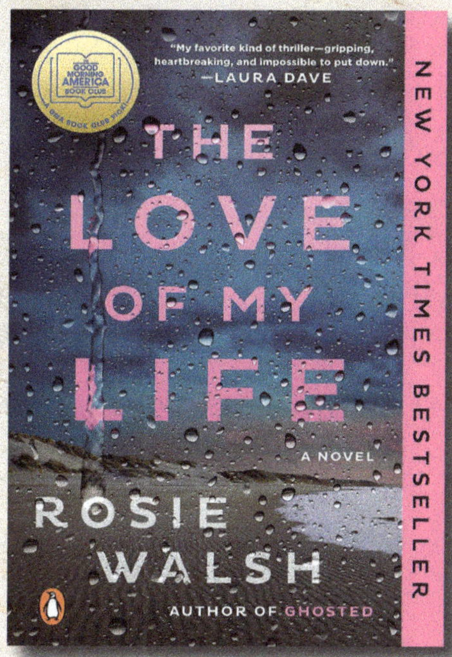

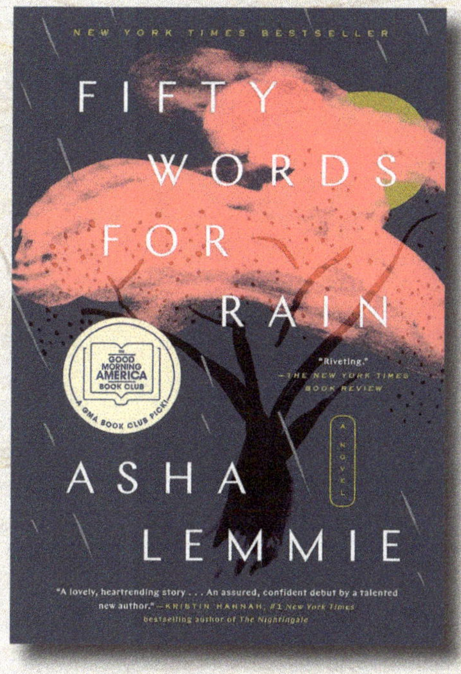

THE PAPER PALACE
by Miranda Cowley Heller

THE LOVE OF MY LIFE
by Rosie Walsh

FIFTY WORDS FOR RAIN
by Asha Lemmie

"A thrilling urban fantasy, 'The Reign of the Occult' captivates with its vivid world, dynamic characters, and relentless action."

Miranda Cowley Heller's debut novel, *The Paper Palace*, is a masterful exploration of love, betrayal, and the complexities of human relationships. Set against the backdrop of a rustic summer retreat in Cape Cod, the story unfolds over a single day, interwoven with flashbacks that span fifty years of the protagonist's life.

The narrative centers on Elle Bishop, who finds herself at a crossroads after a passionate encounter with her childhood friend, Jonas. This moment of infidelity forces Elle to confront her past and the choices that have led her to this pivotal point. Heller's writing is both lyrical and evocative, painting vivid pictures of the natural beauty of the Cape and the emotional landscapes of her characters.

One of the novel's greatest strengths is its rich character development. Elle is a deeply flawed yet relatable protagonist, and her internal struggle is portrayed with raw honesty. The supporting characters, from Elle's charming yet distant husband, Peter, to her enigmatic mother, Wallace, are equally well-drawn, adding depth and complexity to the story.

Heller's use of dual timelines is particularly effective, gradually revealing the secrets and traumas that have shaped Elle's life. This structure keeps the reader engaged, as each revelation adds a new layer of understanding to the present-day narrative. The themes of love, loss, and forgiveness are explored with nuance, making the novel both thought-provoking and emotionally resonant.

However, some readers may find the pacing slow at times, and the frequent shifts between past and present can be disorienting. Despite this, *The Paper Palace* is a compelling read that will linger in your mind long after you've turned the last page. Heller's debut is a testament to her storytelling prowess and a promising start to her literary career.

A beautifully written, emotionally gripping novel that masterfully blends romance and mystery. Rosie Walsh's storytelling is simply unforgettable.

Rosie Walsh's *"The Love of My Life"* is a masterful blend of romance, mystery, and emotional depth that keeps readers hooked from the first page to the last. The novel centers around Emma and Leo, a seemingly perfect couple whose lives are upended when Leo, an obituary writer, discovers startling secrets about Emma's past while researching her life for a piece he hopes never to write.

Walsh's storytelling prowess shines through her intricate plot and well-developed characters. Emma is a compelling protagonist, whose hidden layers are peeled back with each chapter, revealing a complex and relatable woman. Leo's journey from a loving husband to a man grappling with betrayal and confusion is equally gripping. Their relationship, filled with genuine love and palpable tension, forms the heart of the novel.

The narrative is beautifully paced, with Walsh skillfully balancing moments of suspense with poignant reflections on love, trust, and forgiveness. The dual perspectives of Emma and Leo provide a rich, multifaceted view of their relationship and the secrets that threaten to unravel it. Walsh's prose is both lyrical and accessible, making the emotional weight of the story resonate deeply with readers.

One of the standout aspects of *The Love of My Life* is its exploration of identity and the lengths to which people go to protect their loved ones. The twists and turns are expertly crafted, keeping readers guessing until the very end. Walsh's ability to weave a tale that is both heart-wrenching and hopeful is truly commendable.

In summary, *The Love of My Life* is a captivating and emotionally charged novel that showcases Rosie Walsh's talent for creating unforgettable stories. It's a must-read for fans of contemporary fiction and anyone who appreciates a well-told tale of love and redemption.

Fifty Words for Rain is a beautifully written, emotionally gripping tale of resilience, identity, and hope. A truly unforgettable read.

Asha Lemmie's debut novel, "Fifty Words for Rain," is a poignant and beautifully crafted tale that transports readers to post-World War II Japan. The story follows Nori, a biracial child born out of wedlock to a Japanese aristocrat and her African American lover. Abandoned by her mother and left in the care of her strict grandmother, Nori's life is one of confinement and secrecy, reflecting the societal prejudices of the time.

Lemmie's prose is both lyrical and evocative, painting a vivid picture of Nori's internal and external struggles. The author masterfully captures the essence of Nori's resilience and determination as she navigates a world that constantly seeks to diminish her. The character development is exceptional, with Nori's journey from a submissive child to a young woman who dares to dream and defy societal norms being particularly compelling.

The novel's exploration of themes such as identity, family, and the quest for acceptance is both heart-wrenching and inspiring. Lemmie does not shy away from depicting the harsh realities of Nori's life, yet she also infuses the narrative with moments of hope and beauty. The relationship between Nori and her half-brother Akira is especially touching, providing a beacon of light in her otherwise dark world.

Fifty Words for Rain is not just a story about survival; it is a testament to the human spirit's capacity for growth and transformation. Lemmie's ability to weave historical context with a deeply personal story makes this novel a standout. It is a powerful reminder of the importance of perseverance and the enduring quest for self-acceptance.

Asha Lemmie's *Fifty Words for Rain* is a must-read for anyone who appreciates a well-told story of resilience and hope. It is a remarkable debut that promises a bright future for this talented author.

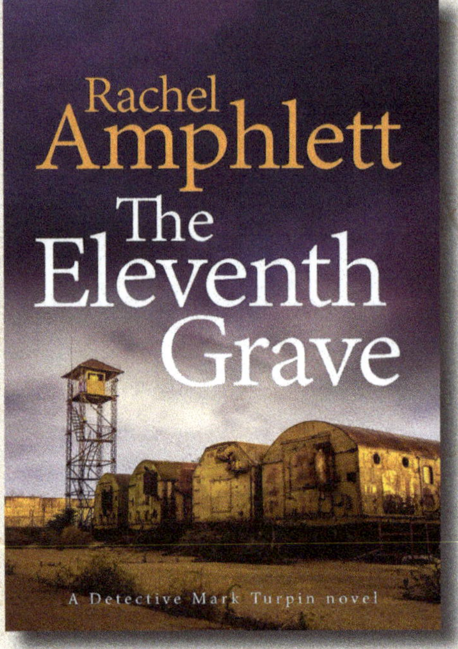

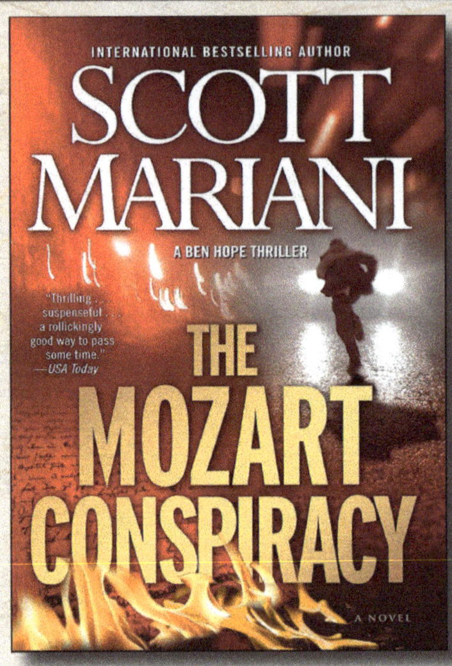

MERELY MORTAL
by *Michelle M. Pillow*

THE ELEVENTH GRAVE
by *Rachel Amphlett*

THE MOZART CONSPIRACY
by *Scott Mariani*

Merely Mortal enchants with its rich world-building, compelling characters, and a beautifully crafted romance. A magical and heartwarming read!

Michelle M. Pillow's *Merely Mortal* is a delightful foray into a world where fantasy and romance intertwine seamlessly. From the very first page, Pillow's masterful storytelling draws readers into a realm filled with magic, intrigue, and heartwarming relationships.

The protagonist, Elara, is a refreshingly relatable character. Her journey from an ordinary life to discovering her extraordinary heritage is both compelling and inspiring. Pillow does an excellent job of developing Elara's character, making her growth feel natural and earned. The supporting characters, particularly the enigmatic and charming Aiden, add depth and richness to the narrative, creating a dynamic ensemble that keeps the reader engaged.

One of the standout aspects of *Merely Mortal* is Pillow's world-building. The magical elements are intricately woven into the fabric of the story, creating a setting that is both fantastical and believable. The author's vivid descriptions and attention to detail make it easy to visualize the enchanting landscapes and mystical creatures that populate this world.

The romance between Elara and Aiden is beautifully crafted, striking a perfect balance between passion and tenderness. Their relationship evolves organically, with moments of tension and vulnerability that add layers to their connection. Pillow's ability to convey deep emotions through her characters is truly commendable.

However, the pacing of the story occasionally feels uneven. Some sections are richly detailed and immersive, while others rush through key plot points, leaving the reader wanting more. Despite this minor flaw, the overall narrative remains engaging and satisfying.

Merely Mortal is a captivating read that will appeal to fans of both fantasy and romance. Michelle M. Pillow has created a magical world that readers will be eager to revisit. With its well-drawn characters and enchanting storyline, this book is a testament to Pillow's talent as a storyteller. Highly recommended for those looking for an escape into a world of magic and love.

A poignant, beautifully written exploration of guilt, redemption, and history's shadows. Boyne's storytelling is both compelling and deeply moving.

Rachel Amphlett's *The Eleventh Grave* is a masterful addition to the Detective Kay Hunter series, delivering a gripping narrative that keeps readers on the edge of their seats from start to finish. Amphlett's skillful storytelling and intricate plotting shine through in this latest installment, making it a must-read for fans of crime thrillers.

The story kicks off with a chilling discovery: a body buried in a shallow grave, with clues that suggest a connection to a series of unsolved murders. Detective Kay Hunter and her team are thrust into a complex investigation that tests their limits and uncovers dark secrets lurking beneath the surface. Amphlett's portrayal of Hunter is both compelling and relatable, as she balances the pressures of her professional life with personal challenges.

One of the standout features of *The Eleventh Grave* is Amphlett's ability to create a palpable sense of tension and urgency. The pacing is impeccable, with each chapter ending on a note that compels you to keep reading. The plot twists are well-executed and keep you guessing until the very end, making it difficult to put the book down.

Amphlett's attention to detail and thorough research are evident in the authenticity of the investigative procedures and the depth of the characters. The supporting cast, including Hunter's colleagues and suspects, are well-developed and add richness to the narrative. The dialogue is sharp and realistic, further immersing readers in the story.

The Eleventh Grave is a stellar addition to the Detective Kay Hunter series. Rachel Amphlett has once again proven her prowess in crafting a suspenseful and engaging thriller. Whether you're a long-time fan of the series or new to Kay Hunter's world, this book is sure to satisfy your craving for a well-written, edge-of-your-seat mystery. Highly recommended.

A masterful blend of history and suspense, "The Mozart Conspiracy" is an unputdownable thriller that captivates from start to finish.

Scott Mariani's "The Mozart Conspiracy" is an exhilarating blend of historical intrigue and modern-day suspense that will captivate readers from the first page to the last. The novel centers around Ben Hope, an ex-SAS operative turned scholar, who is drawn into a centuries-old mystery involving the death of the legendary composer Wolfgang Amadeus Mozart.

Mariani's storytelling prowess shines through in this meticulously researched and vividly described narrative. The historical backdrop of 18th-century Europe is brought to life with rich detail, immersing readers in a world of secret societies, hidden codes, and long-buried secrets. The author skillfully intertwines historical facts with fiction, creating a tapestry of suspense that is both educational and thrilling.

The character of Ben Hope is particularly compelling. Mariani has crafted a protagonist who is not only skilled and resourceful but also deeply human, with personal struggles and vulnerabilities that add depth to his character. Hope's journey is fraught with danger and deception, and his relentless pursuit of the truth makes for a gripping read.

The plot is intricately woven, with numerous twists and turns that keep readers guessing. Just when you think you have it all figured out, Mariani throws in another curveball, maintaining a high level of suspense throughout. The pacing is perfect, with a balance of action-packed sequences and moments of introspection that allow for character development.

"The Mozart Conspiracy" is more than just a thriller; it's a thought-provoking exploration of history, music, and the lengths to which people will go to uncover—or conceal—the truth. Mariani's ability to blend these elements seamlessly is a testament to his skill as a writer.

"The Mozart Conspiracy" is a must-read for fans of historical thrillers and anyone who enjoys a well-crafted mystery. Scott Mariani has delivered a novel that is not only a page-turner but also a richly rewarding reading experience. This book will leave you breathless and eager for more.

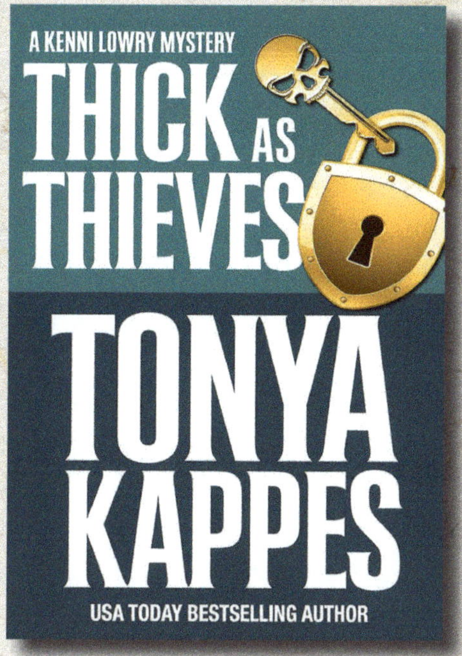

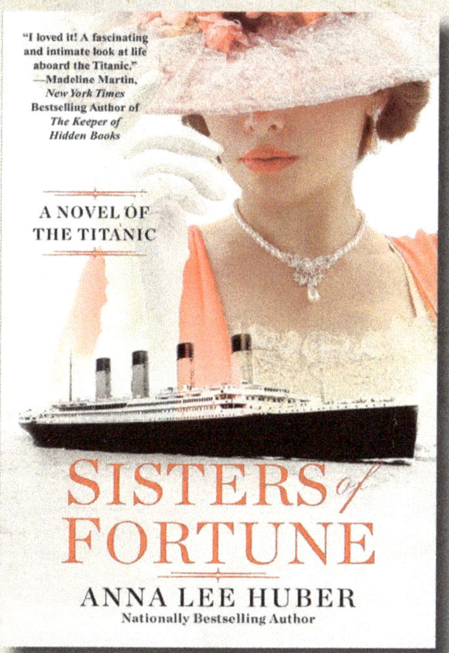

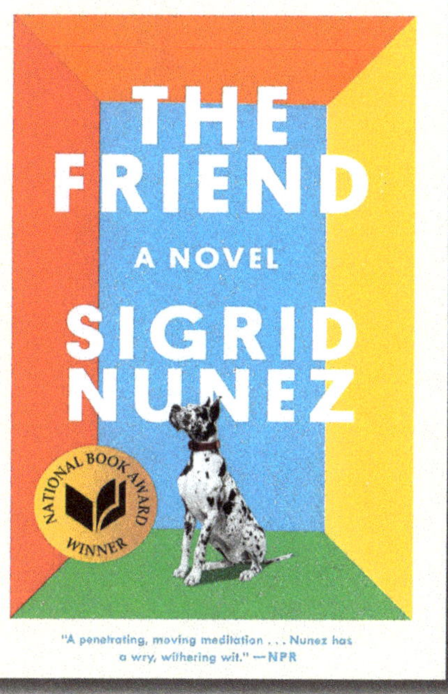

THICK AS THIEVES
by Tonya Kappes

Thick As Thieves is a delightful, suspenseful cozy mystery with charming characters and a captivating Southern setting. Highly recommended!

Thick As Thieves, the latest installment in Tonya Kappes' Kenni Lowry Mystery series, is a delightful blend of Southern charm, humor, and suspense. Set in the quaint town of Cottonwood, Kentucky, this cozy mystery follows Sheriff Kenni Lowry as she navigates a web of secrets, lies, and small-town politics to solve a perplexing murder.

Kappes excels in creating a vivid, engaging setting that feels like a character in its own right. Cottonwood is brought to life with its quirky residents, local gossip, and the ever-present Southern hospitality. The author's attention to detail and her ability to capture the essence of small-town life make the reader feel as though they are part of the community.

Sheriff Kenni Lowry is a compelling protagonist. Her determination, wit, and relatability make her a character readers can root for. The dynamic between Kenni and her ghostly grandfather, Poppa, adds a unique twist to the narrative. Poppa's spectral presence provides both comic relief and valuable insights, making their interactions a highlight of the book.

The plot of *Thick As Thieves* is well-crafted, with enough twists and turns to keep readers guessing until the very end. Kappes skillfully balances the mystery with moments of humor and heart, ensuring that the story remains engaging throughout. The pacing is brisk, and the dialogue is sharp, reflecting the author's knack for capturing the nuances of Southern speech.

One of the strengths of this book is its ensemble cast. The supporting characters are well-developed and add depth to the story. From Kenni's loyal deputy, Finn, to the eccentric townsfolk, each character plays a crucial role in unraveling the mystery.

Thick As Thieves is a thoroughly enjoyable read that will appeal to fans of cozy mysteries and Southern fiction. Tonya Kappes has once again delivered a charming, suspenseful, and heartwarming story that leaves readers eagerly anticipating the next adventure in the Kenni Lowry series.

SISTERS OF FORTUNE
by Anna Lee Huber

Sisters of Fortune is a beautifully crafted historical novel, rich in detail and emotion, with unforgettable characters and gripping plot twists.

Anna Lee Huber's *Sisters of Fortune* is a captivating historical novel that masterfully intertwines mystery, romance, and the complexities of familial bonds. Set against the rich backdrop of 19th-century Europe, the story follows the lives of three sisters—Eleanor, Charlotte, and Georgiana—as they navigate the treacherous waters of society, love, and fortune.

Huber's meticulous attention to historical detail is evident from the very first page, immersing readers in the opulent yet perilous world of the Victorian era. The author's ability to weave historical facts with fiction creates a vivid and believable setting that enhances the narrative's authenticity. The sisters' distinct personalities and their evolving relationships are portrayed with depth and nuance, making them relatable and compelling.

Eleanor, the eldest, is a strong and determined character whose sense of duty often conflicts with her personal desires. Charlotte, the middle sister, is a free spirit whose artistic inclinations and romantic entanglements add layers of intrigue to the plot. Georgiana, the youngest, brings a sense of innocence and curiosity that balances the trio. Their individual journeys are skillfully interwoven, creating a tapestry of suspense and emotional resonance.

The novel's pacing is well-executed, with each chapter revealing new twists and turns that keep readers engaged. Huber's prose is elegant and evocative, capturing the essence of the period while maintaining a modern readability. The themes of sisterhood, loyalty, and the pursuit of happiness are explored with sensitivity and insight, making the story both thought-provoking and heartwarming.

Sisters of Fortune is a testament to Anna Lee Huber's talent as a storyteller. It is a must-read for fans of historical fiction and anyone who appreciates a well-crafted tale of love, mystery, and the enduring bonds of family. This novel is sure to leave a lasting impression and is highly recommended for your next literary adventure.

THE FRIEND
by Sigrid Nunez

A beautifully written, deeply moving exploration of grief, friendship, and healing through an unexpected bond with a Great Dane.

Sigrid Nunez's *The Friend* is a poignant and deeply moving exploration of grief, friendship, and the unexpected ways in which life can offer solace. The novel centers around an unnamed narrator who, after the sudden death of her close friend and mentor, finds herself the reluctant caretaker of his Great Dane, Apollo. As she navigates her profound sense of loss, the bond she forms with the dog becomes a source of unexpected comfort and understanding.

Nunez's prose is both elegant and unflinchingly honest, capturing the complexities of human emotion with a rare sensitivity. The narrative seamlessly weaves together reflections on literature, the nature of writing, and the intricacies of human relationships, creating a rich tapestry that resonates on multiple levels. The relationship between the narrator and Apollo is depicted with such tenderness and authenticity that it transcends the typical pet-owner dynamic, becoming a profound meditation on companionship and healing.

The novel delves into the narrator's internal struggles, her memories of her friend, and her reflections on the literary world, all while she grapples with the challenges of caring for a dog that is as large as he is gentle. Apollo, with his silent yet powerful presence, becomes a mirror to the narrator's own journey through grief, offering her a sense of purpose and a new perspective on life.

The Friend is not just a story about loss; it is also a celebration of the enduring power of love and the ways in which it can manifest in our lives. Nunez's ability to convey the depth of her characters' inner worlds makes this novel a deeply affecting read that lingers long after the final page. The book is a testament to the healing power of companionship, whether it comes from a human or an animal, and it beautifully illustrates how connections can help us navigate the darkest times.

From Investigator to Novelist

Robert Emmers' diverse career shapes his action-filled, existential fiction, blending investigative experiences with disciplined storytelling.

How a Career in Journalism and Private Investigation Fuels Thrilling Fiction

Robert Emmers masterfully transforms real-life adventures into captivating fiction, offering readers thrilling narratives and profound existential themes.

Acclaimed author Robert Emmers is a man whose life reads like a novel, filled with vivid stories and extraordinary experiences. As a teenager, Emmers dreamed of writing in Paris, but practicality led him into journalism. His career path was anything but conventional, taking him through roles as a private investigator, insurance fraud detective, and crisis communications specialist. These varied experiences have now become the rich backdrop for his fiction. From evading federal subpoenas and facing threats from mob figures to chasing fugitives and surveilling rogue priests, Emmers has done it all. Today, he resides in the tranquil woods of northwest Pennsylvania, focusing on his passion for writing.

In his latest works, *The Secret History* and the short story *Where Did All the Dentists Go?*, Emmers showcases his ability to blend action-packed narratives with deeper existential themes. His writing is a reflection of his diverse career, filled with the thrill of past escapades and the disciplined, concise style honed in newsrooms.

In an exclusive interview, Emmers opens up about how his eclectic career has shaped his storytelling and writing style, the inspirations behind his dark and complex themes, and his journey back to fiction.

When asked how his diverse professional experiences have influenced his writing, Emmers attributes his concise style to his journalism background, drawing a parallel to Hemingway's clean writing. However, he emphasizes that the action and confrontation inherent in his investigative work have had an even more significant impact on his fiction, ensuring there's always an element of excitement and movement.

The Secret History delves into themes of government death squads, crime, and vengeance. Emmers explains that the novel was born out of his work in crisis communication, particularly his role as a fixer on the streets. Originally an unpublished novel featuring a character named Dahl, the story evolved from a short story into a full novel, set in Mexico—a place he loves. The scenes are a mix of personal experiences and imaginative embellishments.

His short story, *Where Did All the Dentists Go?*, began with a simple, magical first line and transformed into a narrative inspired by the Japanese phenomenon of johatsu, where people leave their lives and disappear. Emmers mentions that he doesn't consciously worry about themes but acknowledges that a recurring theme in his writing is the idea of constant movement—forward or backward—never standing still.

Drawing parallels between his protagonist's search for answers and his own journey as a writer, Emmers reflects on his life as an exploration. His varied careers mirror the quests of his characters, all of whom are seeking answers in their own ways. In *The Secret History*, for instance, the main characters, despite being despicable, are intriguing due to their relentless search for answers.

Balancing intricate plots with existential themes, Emmers prefers the freedom of short stories over the structured approach required for novels. He enjoys the spontaneity of short stories, where a single line can spark an entire narrative, allowing the plot to unfold organically. Novels, on the other hand, require meticulous construction and an outline, although even those plans can change as characters take control of their destinies. His preferred theme in novels is seeking redemption and moving forward.

Emmers is drawn to unconventional settings and characters, often writing about drunks, screw-ups, and people in bizarre situations. This fascination stems partly from the contrast with his relatively conventional life as a writer. Through his characters, he explores worlds far removed from his own, creating immersive and compelling fictional realms. Writing allows him to inhabit the minds of crooks and weirdos, compensating for his desk-bound reality.

Robert Emmers' stories, whether set in the dangerous streets of Mexico or a mysterious village, offer readers a glimpse into a world of action, intrigue, and existential questioning. His ability to draw from his own adventurous past and infuse it with imagination makes his fiction both gripping and thought-provoking. As he continues to write, Emmers invites readers to join him on journeys that echo the excitement and discovery of his own life.

> *My life has been an exploration. Probably that's why I've had so many different (and always fun) careers. The idea of exploration carries over into my fiction. Every character is looking for answers. For example, in The Secret History, all of the main characters are pretty despicable. But what makes them interesting to me is that they're all looking for answers, of one sort or another. "*

Robert Emmers

From Personal Fears to Page-Turners

Christina McDonald shares her inspirations, creative process, and personal experiences that shape her bestselling thrillers, offering insights into her characters, cultural influences, and journalistic background.

How Christina McDonald Crafts Her Stories

Christina McDonald, a USA Today bestselling author, has captivated readers worldwide with her intricately woven thrillers that blend suspense, mystery, and deep emotional undertones. With titles like *What Lies In Darkness, The Stranger At Black Lake,* and *Do No Harm*, McDonald has solidified her place in the literary world. We caught up with her to delve into the inspirations behind her gripping narratives, her creative process, and how her personal experiences shape her writing.

The Genesis of a Thriller Author

From an early age, Christina McDonald was enamored with stories that made her heart race and her mind whirl. Growing up in Seattle, she was an avid reader, devouring mystery series like Nancy Drew and The Hardy Boys. These early influences sparked a lifelong fascination with the thriller genre. "*I think that thrillers tap into our deepest fears, that dissonance between real life and 'what if',*" McDonald shares. "*Exploring the darker side of humanity provides a certain catharsis, I think, the ability to allay those fears, to ultimately find closure.*"

McDonald's approach to creating compelling narratives revolves around the delicate balance between character and plot. She emphasizes the importance of crafting characters that readers can emotionally connect with and root for, stating, "*I always start with a concept that is immediately so interesting that I can't turn away from it. And then I create my character(s).*"

Personal Connections and Authentic Narratives

McDonald's upcoming thriller, *What Lies In Darkness*, is a deeply personal story rooted in a recurring nightmare she has experienced. The chilling premise of coming home to find her entire family missing became the foundation of the novel. "*Instead of turning away from it, like I usually did, I leaned in and started writing about it,*" McDonald reveals. This personal touch extends to her characters, making them resonate deeply with readers.

The Evolution of Jess Lambert

In her novella *The Stranger At Black Lake*, McDonald introduces readers to Jess Lambert, a character who evolved from a secondary role to the protagonist of her own series. Initially intended as a way to put pressure on another character, Jess quickly became a focal point. McDonald's editor suggested making Jess the main character, leading to a significant rewrite and a deeper exploration of her backstory and motivations. "*Jess's internal arc is about grief, so each book in the series shows how she's not only solving cases in her job as a detective, but how she's moving through those stages of grief,*" McDonald explains.

Cultural Influences and Journalistic Roots

Having lived in both the United States and the United Kingdom, McDonald's experiences in different cultures have enriched her storytelling. "*Living in different countries and learning about different cultures has taught me to be more open-minded,*" she says. This open-mindedness and curiosity are evident in her writing, adding depth and diversity to her characters and settings.

With an MA in Journalism from the National University of Ireland, Galway, McDonald's journalistic background has honed her ability to find the heart of a story. "*Having a background in journalism has trained me to look for the plot of my story, and to ask: why do I care? Why will my reader care?*" she notes. This investigative mindset is crucial for crafting compelling thrillers, where uncovering the truth is often central to the plot.

Tackling Tough Topics

In *Do No Harm*, McDonald addresses the sensitive issue of opioid addiction, drawing from personal experiences with her brother's struggle. Her research was extensive, involving interviews with various experts and a deep dive into the opioid epidemic. McDonald hopes the book highlights the real cost of addiction and the complexity of moral dilemmas it presents. "*Even good people can get addicted to bad things,*" she emphasizes, aiming to shed light on the human side of the crisis.

The Creative Process

McDonald's writing process is driven by what she describes as the "*aura of the story.*" This strong sense of urgency propels her to write, even if the initial feeling isn't always clear. "*From there, it's really about showing up every day and writing scene after scene until I have a full book,*" she says. This disciplined approach helps her navigate the challenges of writer's block and maintain a steady creative flow.

Christina McDonald's thrillers are a testament to her ability to weave intricate plots with deep emotional resonance. Her personal experiences, journalistic training, and cultural insights converge to create stories that not only entertain but also provoke thought and connection. As readers eagerly await the release of *What Lies In Darkness*, they can be assured of another gripping journey into the complexities of human fears and relationships.

Christina McDonald, USA Today bestselling author known for her gripping thrillers, shares insights into her creative process and personal inspirations.

> *Living in different countries and learning about different cultures has taught me to be more open-minded. It has shown me that there are so many perspectives, so many 'right' ways of doing things, and that being open and curious about them enriches my stories."*

Christina McDonald

Exploring Love and Loss in The Yellow Rose

Janice Angelique, a versatile author, draws inspiration from her diverse background and life experiences, writing across multiple genres and embracing sel

Celebrating Jamaican Heritage through Fiction

Janice Angelique's life story is as rich and diverse as the novels she pens. Born in Jamaica, West Indies, she moved to Brooklyn, New York, in 1970 to reunite with her mother. Her journey from Erasmus Hall High School to becoming an acclaimed author is a testament to her resilience and creativity. Now residing in South Florida with her husband and their bossy poodle, Tippa, Janice continues to draw inspiration from her life experiences, including her marriage and extensive travels.

Janice's literary career is marked by her refusal to be confined to a single genre. As a self-published author, she has written over ten romance novels, two fantasy novels, three poetry books, and three children's books. While four of her romance novels were traditionally published, Janice found that self-publishing offered her the freedom to explore and push boundaries. This decision was partly driven by her frustration with the traditional publishing industry's gatekeeping, where a single rejection could halt her progress. Despite this, she remains open to traditional publishing and is currently working on her memoir, *A Little Bitter Sweet Memoir*.

Cloud Cover and The Yellow Rose

The loss of her sister Aster in 1999 was a pivotal moment for Janice, profoundly influencing her writing. The sudden and devastating nature of Aster's death left a void that Janice sought to fill through her novels. *The Yellow Rose*, written in 2006, and *Cloud Cover*, penned in 2010, are two such works that reflect her emotional journey.

The Yellow Rose was inspired by the Iraq war and its impact on Americans. Although Janice had no direct connection to the war, the senseless loss of young soldiers deeply affected her. The novel tells the story of Leopold, a young Caucasian professor from Princeton University, who falls in love with Rosalyn, a Jamaican waitress. Both characters are marked by loss—Leopold's wife died in a car accident, and Rosalyn's husband was killed in the Iraq war. Their relationship, fraught with challenges, ultimately becomes a tale of mutual protection and healing. Janice's personal experiences in Princeton, where she lived for five years, provided the authentic backdrop for this poignant story.

Cloud Cover, later renamed "A New Dawning" in 2022 due to publishing errors, draws on Janice's relationships with family and friends. Set in the San Fernando Valley, California, where she lived for fourteen years, the novel explores themes of bigotry and perseverance. The story was influenced by her OBGYN's experiences growing up in Watts, a notoriously violent area in Los Angeles. Through the character of Masie, Janice delves into the prejudices that can arise from one's place of birth, highlighting the strength and determination required to overcome such biases.

The Other Side of the Mountain

Published in 2011 by Genesis Press, "The Other Side of the Mountain" transports readers to the Blue Mountains of Jamaica. This novel delves into the lives of the fabled Rahjah Rastafarians, a community Janice created in her first book, "Angel's Paradise." By portraying a peaceful, knowledgeable, and romantic side of Rastafarian culture, Janice challenges common misconceptions. Her time spent in the Blue Mountains provided the serene and tranquil setting for this intimate and imaginative story.

The Path to Self-Publishing

Janice's decision to self-publish was driven by her desire for creative freedom and her frustration with the traditional publishing industry's limitations. While her traditionally published books came with numerous stipulations, self-publishing allowed her to experiment and innovate. However, she acknowledges the challenges of self-publishing, particularly in marketing. Despite these hurdles, Janice emphasizes the importance of producing high-quality work, underscoring the necessity of hiring a good editor.

Elements of Jamaica

Janice's Jamaican heritage is a significant influence on her writing. Growing up in Jamaica, she encountered respected Rastafarians who were professors and patrons of the arts. These individuals inspired her to create the Rahjah Rastafarians, a fictional community that showcases the peaceful, knowledgeable, and reputable aspects of Rastafarian culture. Through her novels, Janice aims to bring awareness to this often misunderstood culture, highlighting its strength and romanticism.

Janice Angelique's literary journey is a testament to her versatility and dedication. Her ability to draw from her diverse background and life experiences has resulted in a body of work that resonates with readers across genres and continents. As she continues to write and explore new themes, Janice remains a powerful voice in the world of literature.

> *Janice Angelique's storytelling is a masterful blend of imagination and authenticity, making her a standout voice in contemporary literature.*

> *I am a Jamaican living in the USA for many years. Growing up in Jamaica, I met a few respected Rastafarians who were professors, patron of the arts, etc. They inspired me. I created the Rahjah Rastafarians to bring awareness to a different side of the culture— the peaceful, knowledgeable, strong, reputable, romantic side of this culture."*

Janice Angelique

Navigating Life's Challenges Through Fiction

S.M. Stevens discusses her transition from business to fiction writing, inspired by personal health crises, and her commitment to addressing societal issues through her novels.

S.M. Stevens on Writing, Resilience, and Representation

S.M. Stevens transitioned from a business writer to a fiction author following two health crises. After a horseback riding accident left her on crutches, she wrote *Shannon's Odyssey* for her younger daughter. A year later, during chemotherapy for ovarian cancer, she penned *Bit Players, Has-Been Actors and Other Posers* for her older daughter. Post-recovery, she continued writing, producing the *Bit Players* series and her first adult novel, *Horseshoes and Hand Grenades*, inspired by the #metoo movement. Stevens' next novel, *Beautiful and Terrible Things*, releases in summer 2024.

Acclaimed author S.M. Stevens has carved a niche for herself in contemporary fiction by tackling complex societal issues such as workplace harassment, mental health struggles, and social justice. Her novels are not just stories but reflections of real-life challenges, filled with humor, light, and love. Stevens' approach to writing is deeply rooted in her desire to provoke thought and inspire empathy among her readers.

Stevens' upcoming novel, *Beautiful and Terrible Things*, is a testament to her commitment to depicting contemporary society with all its multifaceted issues. Set in a modern American city, the novel explores themes of friendship, mental illness, and social justice. Stevens hopes that readers will come away with a greater understanding and empathy for the real people behind the statistics, and perhaps feel inspired to engage more deeply with causes that matter to them.

Her extensive career in corporate communications has significantly influenced her writing process. Stevens learned to write amidst constant interruptions, a skill that has served her well in balancing her professional and personal life. This ability to maintain focus and productivity in short bursts has undoubtedly contributed to her prolific output.

In her novel *Horseshoes and Hand Grenades*, Stevens merges the topics of childhood sexual abuse and workplace sexual harassment, drawing parallels between the societal responses to both. The novel was partly inspired by the #metoo movement, which highlighted the pervasive nature of harassment and the often dismissive questions victims face. Stevens' narrative seeks to address these questions and provide a voice to those who have been silenced.

Representation in literature is a crucial aspect of Stevens' work. She emphasizes the importance of research and sensitivity in crafting authentic and diverse characters. For *Beautiful and Terrible Things*, she consulted with numerous sensitivity readers and drew on the experiences of individuals from various backgrounds to ensure her characters were three-dimensional and believable.

Stevens' *Bit Player*s series, inspired by her daughter's love for musical theatre, showcases her ability to write for a younger audience. Her personal experiences as a parent and volunteer in school theatre programs are reflected in the series. The biggest challenge she faced was ensuring her writing did not embarrass her teenage daughter, a concern that led to the creation of her pen name.

S.M. Stevens' novels are a blend of entertainment and thought-provoking themes, offering readers a mirror to society's complexities. Her dedication to authenticity and representation, combined with her ability to balance serious subjects with engaging storytelling, makes her a standout voice in contemporary fiction.

The greatest impact my communications career had on my fiction-writing career was teaching me how to write with constant interruptions. I learned to write in five-minute increments—literally, and to not lose focus, despite multiple interruptions from my staff and my boss. That carried over to interruptions from the family and the dogs when writing at home."

S. M. Stevens

Crafting Thrills and Chills

D.M. Foley discusses her journey from educator to acclaimed author, her inspirations, and the themes explored in her psychological thrillers, including the award-winning Lyons Garden Trilogy.

BY BEN ALAN

An Inside Look at the Foley's Inspirations and Writing Process

D.M. Foley's literary journey has been nothing short of remarkable. Her debut novel, *The Lyons Garden Book One: Family Ties*, garnered favorable reviews and was awarded The New York Best Sellers Gold Award in December 2021. The success continued with her second book, *Erasing Secrets: The Lyons Garden Book Two*, which received several 5-star reviews. The trilogy concluded with *Pawns: The Lyons Garden Book Three*, released on September 13, 2022, and it too has been met with acclaim.

Residing in Southeastern Connecticut with her husband, three sons, and her mother, Foley draws inspiration from her local surroundings, often incorporating familiar places into her narratives. Before becoming a full-time author, she worked as a preschool teacher and later as a paraeducator, roles that allowed her to instill a love of reading and writing in her students. Her academic background includes an Associate's Degree in Early Childhood Education and a Bachelor's Degree in Liberal Studies with a concentration in Early Childhood Education and Human Development.

The Pen Name Decision

Choosing to write under a pen name to protect her family's anonymity, Foley found this decision had minimal impact on her writing journey. The primary adjustment was transitioning her personal social media presence to her pen name to avoid well-meaning friends and family tagging her personal pages in posts about her books.

A Turning Point in the Pandemic

The global pandemic served as a pivotal moment in Foley's writing career. After losing her father in January 2020 and resigning from her paraeducator position in September 2020 to assist her youngest son with hybrid learning, she found herself with the time to complete a story she had started in 2017. This story became *Family Ties: The Lyons Garden Book One*.

Inspiration Behind The Lyons Garden Series

Foley's first book was inspired by her genealogy research, which revealed a connection between her husband and Lion Gardener of Gardener's Island. This discovery sparked her imagination, leading her to explore the potential consequences of an unknown heir being found. The series delves into themes of found family, friendship, family relationships, grief, and the unintended consequences of actions.

The Killer Trip: A High School Adventure Turned Thriller

The Killer Trip was born from a challenge by two of Foley's best friends to write a story based on a high school trip they took together.

Incorporating real events, Foley crafted a psychological thriller where a past trip has significant repercussions in the present. The storyline, which includes a made-up scenario of one of the friends being arrested for a murder they didn't commit, has resonated with readers and is Foley's favorite work to date. A sequel is in the works, exploring the aftermath of the protagonist Laney Wilson's experiences.

Exploring Fantastical Elements in Deric Dream Changer

Deric Dream Changer introduces the concept of controlling dreams to alter outcomes, inspired by Foley's own experiences with anxiety and vivid nightmares. The book explores psychic abilities and their potential to save lives and perform good deeds. Readers have compared the character of Deric to Dean Koontz's Odd Thomas and noted similarities to *Final Destination*. Foley describes it as a mix of *Hardy Boys* meets *Stranger Things*. The second book in the series, *Adeline Astral Warrior*, is expected to be released by the end of 2024 or early 2025.

Crafting Suspense in Pawns: The Lyons Garden Book Three

The final installment of The Lyons Garden Trilogy, *Pawns*, involves a thrilling game of cat-and-mouse between the Gardiner family and a killer. Foley builds suspense through the use of red herrings, cliffhangers, and multiple plot twists, ensuring a gripping conclusion to the series.

D.M. Foley's ability to weave intricate plots and build suspense has solidified her place in the psychological thriller genre. With several ideas for future books in various genres, her readers eagerly await what she will create next. Follow her on social media to stay updated on her latest projects.

D.M. Foley captivates readers with her intricate plots, compelling characters, and masterful suspense, solidifying her place in psychological thrillers.

> *The turning point in my writing career came during the global pandemic. I lost my Dad in January 2020, and I resigned from my paraeducator position in September 2020 to help my youngest son navigate the world of hybrid learning. This gave me extra time on my hands, and I committed to finish writing a story I had started in 2017. That story became Family Ties: The Lyons Garden Book One."*

D.M. Foley

Mystery, and Love in Regency Romances

Victoria Chatham discusses blending historical settings with romance and mystery, her transition to contemporary westerns, and offers advice for aspiring authors, emphasizing research and community involvement.

Finding Inspiration in Books and Movies

Victoria Chatham, an acclaimed author known for her captivating tales of lords, ladies, and the intricacies of manners and wit, has carved a niche for herself in the world of romantic historical novels. Published by BWL Publishing Inc., Chatham's works are available in both e-book and print formats. Her journey into the literary world began with writing articles and short stories for magazines and online forums, eventually leading her to the realm of Regency romances. Despite an editor once telling her she was "too English" to write a western, Chatham also ventured into contemporary western romance, proving her versatility as a writer.

Chatham's novels often blend historical settings with elements of romance and mystery. When asked about this unique combination, she explains, "I like to give my characters a little more to deal with than simply boy meets girl. With my Regency novels, I first decide in which year I'm going to set my story, then look for historical events that happened during that year and decide how my characters can be involved in them or how those happenings can affect my characters."

One of her notable works, "Brides of Banff Springs," is part of a series celebrating Canada's 150th birthday, featuring stories set in different provinces and territories. Chatham incorporated historical events and locations into the narrative while crafting a compelling romance. "The premise for this collection was for the stories to be historically accurate and the romance suitable for readers thirteen years old and upwards. As an occasional visitor to Banff, I didn't know much about the town's history, but once I started my research, I collected a wealth of material. This book is set in 1935, so I had to ensure all the information I included was accurate to that date or before. Once I had a feasible timeline, I created the characters and worked them into the story," she shares.

Chatham's "Those Regency Belles" series follows the romantic adventures of different heroines in the Regency era. Her inspiration for this time period stems from her childhood in Clifton, Bristol, where the Regency architecture captivated her. "I loved the graceful outlines of the crescents and the grand houses. As a teenager, I started reading Georgette Heyer's Regency romance novels and wanted to tell similar stories. Keeping my characters within the restraints of historical accuracy is a challenge. I believe that there have been extraordinary people in every era, many of whom have rebelled against or ignored the social mores of the day. I like my characters to be on the feisty side and hope they give my readers a reason to turn the page," she explains.

Transitioning from historical romance to contemporary western romance with titles like "Loving That Cowboy" and "Legacy of Love," Chatham was motivated by her fascination with the West and cowboy culture. "I've lived in Canada for over thirty years now, and my Western romances are an homage to that culture. The switch came when I pitched a premise to an editor at a writers' conference in Calgary, Alberta, who told me I was too English to write a contemporary Western romance. I had read many novels in that genre and thought I could. I wanted to prove her wrong, and both 'Loving That Cowboy' and 'Legacy of Love' were well enough received that I wrote a third, 'Loving Georgia Caldwell,' released in February of this year. I quickly discovered that I needed to do as much research for my contemporary Western romances as for the historical novels. I've interviewed ranchers, working cowboys and girls, stock contractors and rodeo performers. Some of my questions raised eyebrows, if not outright laughter, but were respectfully answered, and all gave authenticity to my imaginary ranch settings," she recounts.

As an active member of Romance Writers of America and the Calgary Association of Romance Writers of America, Chatham credits these communities for significantly influencing her writing journey. "For me, achieving publication would have taken much longer had it not been for my involvement with both organizations. As a new writer, they gave me the support I needed. Regarding advice for aspiring romance authors, I would encourage anyone to join a good writing group. You will find like-minded people with whom you can discuss ideas and brainstorm plots and characters. There is a big gap between being a reader and understanding all the elements of the craft of writing as an author. Attending workshops and conferences is also a great way to meet other authors, agents, and editors. There is so much on the internet these days on how to write novels in various genres, but there is still nothing quite like that personal contact, especially if you are fortunate enough to meet your favourite author," she advises.

Beyond writing, Chatham enjoys reading and watching movies for inspiration and escapism. She shares, "Watching movies is a great way to learn the 'how to' of pacing, tension, and especially subtext. I've always liked Lee Child's Jack Reacher books, and now the TV series, for how he sets up his fight scenes. The Mission Impossible and Die Hard movies are great examples of pacing and tension. LA Confidential, set in 1950s Los Angeles, has great lines of subtext between two of the characters, Lynn Bracken and Officer 'Bud' White. Mary Balogh is another writer of Regency romances that I admire, as is Jo Goodman, who writes both Regency and Western romances."

Victoria Chatham's dedication to her craft and her ability to seamlessly blend history, mystery, and love make her a standout author in the romance genre. Her stories not only transport readers to different eras but also offer a rich tapestry of characters and events that keep them turning the pages.

> " *I like to give my characters a little more to deal with than simply boy meets girl. With my Regency novels, I first decide in which year I'm going to set my story, then look for historical events that happened during that year and decide how my characters can be involved in them or how those happenings can affect my characters.*"

Victoria Chatham

Overcoming Self-Doubt with Just Say It

Yorkshire-born Tessa Barrie transitioned from poetry to novels, overcoming self-doubt and embracing her heritage, humor, and life experiences in her writing.

Advice for Aspiring Writers. Seize the Moment

Yorkshire-born Tessa Barrie had her first taste of literary success in her early teens with the publication of her poetry. After leaving school, she ventured into freelance writing for newspapers and magazines. However, the financial instability of freelancing soon necessitated a shift to a more traditional job. Despite the demands of full-time employment, Tessa's passion for writing never waned. She continued to write in various forms, from short stories to magazine fillers, and even dabbled in songwriting.

In June 2021, Tessa self-published her debut novel, *Just Say It*. Reflecting on her journey, she admits she wishes she had started writing novels earlier. The first draft of *Just Say It* was completed in her thirties, but self-doubt delayed its publication. Now, she believes that starting later in life has made her more driven, as she recognizes the importance of seizing the moment and not procrastinating.

Tessa's dream of living by the sea came true in 1981 when she moved to Jersey in the Channel Islands. Now retired, she splits her time between Jersey and Portugal, dedicating most of her time to writing.

Tessa's Yorkshire

heritage has significantly influenced her writing, particularly in capturing the bittersweet essence of life with humor. Born in Harrogate, she moved south at the age of three but remains proud of her Yorkshire roots. The straightforward, no-nonsense attitude of Yorkshire folk, coupled with their subtle and dry sense of humor, is deeply ingrained in her. Tessa recalls her formative years as a blend of emotional disturbances and humor, which helped heal and navigate through life's challenges.

Just Say It delves into themes of familial relationships and self-discovery. Tessa acknowledges that all authors draw on their own experiences. While her main character, Lisa, shares some similarities with Tessa's own life, such as spending time in Portugal, the story is not autobiographical. The character of Lisa's mother, Elizabeth, is inspired by Tessa's late mother, but their stories diverge significantly.

Incorporating humor into writing can be challenging, but Tessa strives to balance the bittersweet moments with comedic elements. With only one self-published novel to her credit, she admits she still has much to learn about technique. However,

with her second novel finished and a third in progress, she hopes her skills are improving.

Tessa's forthcoming novel, *The Secret Lives of the Doyenne of Didsbrook*, started as a humorous short story about a writers' group in a remote UK village. The story evolved into a quirky murder mystery as the characters developed and became more complex. Tessa rewrote the novel several times, shifting from slapstick scenarios to a more bittersweet approach. The novel is currently going through the submission process.

Cassie, Tessa's feisty Shorkie, has been a constant companion and source of inspiration, especially during challenging times like Lockdown. Although Cassie's blogging career has taken a back seat since Tessa started writing novels, her presence continues to be a source of joy and motivation.

For those hesitant to pursue their passion for writing, Tessa offers simple yet powerful advice: "Don't wait - just write!" She encourages aspiring writers to join writers' groups, attend workshops, and seek help from fellow writers. Building confidence and taking that leap of faith is crucial. Tessa emphasizes the importance of overcoming self-doubt and getting your work out into the world.

Tessa Barrie's journey from poetry to prose is a testament to the power of perseverance and the importance of following one's passion, no matter the stage of life. Her story is an inspiration to aspiring writers everywhere.

> One of the reviewers for Just Say It mentions that it reads like an autobiography... of sorts. All authors draw on their own experiences. Of course, they do. I was brought up in Gloucestershire, and these days, I spend a great deal of time in Portugal, as does my main character, Lisa, in Just Say It. My mother and I were polar opposites, so Lisa's mother, Elizabeth, does share a few of my late mother's character traits, but that is where it ends. Elizabeth's story is very far removed from my mother's.

Tessa Barrie

Tessa Barrie's writing is a delightful blend of humor and heartfelt storytelling, making her an inspiring and captivating author.

Mystery, and Love in Regency Romances

Karen Nappa, an Amazon bestselling author, writes realistic BDSM romance inspired by personal experiences, emphasizing Safe, Sane, and Consensual practices. Her stories balance romance, suspense, and authentic relationship dynamics.

An Insight into the Life and Writing of an Amazon Bestselling Author

Karen Nappa, an Amazon bestselling author, has been captivating readers with her seasoned BDSM romance novels since 2019. Her works, including the popular series "Small-Town Submission" and "Doms in Uniform," are known for their realistic and romantic portrayal of the D/s lifestyle. Living in the Netherlands with her dominant husband, children, and two Chausie cats, Karen's life is as vibrant and dynamic as the stories she writes. When she's not writing, she enjoys reading, kickboxing, and listening to heavy metal.

Karen's personal experiences in the D/s lifestyle significantly influence her writing. She shares, "Most of the BDSM scenes in my books (if not all) are based on personal experiences. I know the freedom of being bound, I've experienced subspace, and I've tried many impact toys (I really, really don't like canes)." This authenticity allows her to create scenes that are both realistic and relatable for readers familiar with the lifestyle. Her emphasis on Safe, Sane, and Consensual (SSC) practices ensures that her stories, even when they start with unconventional relationships, maintain a foundation of trust and respect.

The inspiration behind Karen's series often stems from her personal journey and professional challenges. "When I started writing, it was with a publisher who turned out to be less than trustworthy. Along with dozens of other authors, we fled 'the Woodshed' and most of us turned indie," she explains. This led to the creation of the "Small Town Submission" series, an interconnected family saga with a dark secret. The "Savage Billionaires" series marked another significant shift in her career, especially after her co-author Ellen decided to quit writing. Joining Red Hot Romance Ink, Karen embarked on this new project, continuing to explore and expand her storytelling.

Writing romance with a BDSM theme comes with its own set of challenges and rewards. Karen notes, "A big challenge for me is that I write erotic romance, and because of the BDSM element in my books, it's often mistaken for erotica. I have nothing against erotica, I just don't write it." Her focus is on relationship-driven narratives where sex and BDSM are integral to the characters' connection. The reward lies in depicting the depth and complexity of these relationships and the trust involved in BDSM dynamics.

Balancing the sensual and romantic aspects of her stories with elements of suspense and drama is something Karen does with finesse. "The backbone of my story is the relationship, and the sensual parts help move that connection along," she says. Influenced by authors like Colin Forbes, Alistair MacLean, and Desmond Bagley, Karen weaves suspense into her plots, ensuring that the romance and drama complement each other seamlessly.

Through her books, Karen hopes to provide readers with a realistic view of BDSM relationships. She also aims to encourage older women to explore their sexuality and kinks. "Life doesn't end after 40 (or 50 or 60), and you don't have to be a 20-something virgin to discover new and exciting things about yourself," she asserts.

Karen's writing process is a blend of planning and spontaneity. "I'm a mix between a plotter and a pantser. I always start out my stories with a solid outline. About halfway through each manuscript, my characters act up. They don't listen, they get a mind of their own, and they have me running in circles," she shares. This dynamic process often leads her to skip forward to the epilogue, giving her and her characters a clear destination for their happily ever after.

Karen Nappa's journey as an author is as compelling as the stories she writes. Her dedication to authenticity, her ability to balance romance and suspense, and her encouragement for readers to explore their own desires make her a standout voice in the world of BDSM romance.

Karen Nappa masterfully blends authenticity and romance, creating compelling BDSM stories that resonate deeply with readers. A truly exceptional author.

> *A big challenge for me is that I write erotic romance, and because of the BDSM element in my books, it's often mistaken for erotica. I have nothing against erotica, I just don't write it. My books are mainly relationship-driven; however, my characters use sex and BDSM to cement that relationship, and they don't close the bedroom (or dungeon, kitchen, etc.) door.*

Karen Nappa

Lake Arrowhead's Inspiration

Chrysteen Braun's diverse career and life experiences inspire her novels, blending historical fiction, romance, and mystery, set against the backdrop of Lake Arrowhead's serene mountains.

The Setting Behind the "Cabin" Novels

Award-winning author Chrysteen Braun, a native Californian, has led a life as diverse and rich as the stories she pens. Born and raised in Long Beach, Chrysteen's journey into the world of writing began at the tender age of twelve with her first novel. Although the details of that early work have faded, the dream of becoming a writer never left her.

At eighteen, Chrysteen found herself amidst the vibrant chaos of Hollywood, working for Capitol Records. Her task? Ordering album covers for the Beatles' iconic "Sgt. Pepper's Lonely Hearts Club Band." Despite her initial skepticism about the song "Lucy in the Sky with Diamonds," this experience was just one of many that would later color her writing.

When career decisions loomed, Chrysteen joined her family's construction business, eventually becoming a licensed flooring and general contractor. For nearly fifty years, she and her husband Larry dedicated themselves to remodeling and interior design, a legacy now carried on by their daughter. Yet, the call to write never truly faded.

In the early 1980s, Chrysteen rekindled her passion for writing by joining an Orange County writers' group alongside then-unknown author Elizabeth George. Although life and business took precedence, she continued to write articles on remodeling and interior design for local newspapers. Retirement offered Chrysteen the perfect opportunity to reinvent herself and dive back into the world of fiction.

A member of the Southern California Writers Association and OC Romance Writers, Chrysteen draws inspiration from her second home in Lake Arrowhead, California. Here, she opened a home decor store aptly named *At The Cabin,* and the serene mountain setting became the backdrop for her *Cabin* novels.

Chrysteen currently resides in Coto de Caza, California, with her husband Larry, whom she affectionately calls "the wind beneath my wings." Her journey from a young girl with a dream to an accomplished author is a testament to the enduring power of passion and perseverance.

Reflecting on her early writing experiences, Chrysteen recalls, "I wish I still had that novel, although I'm sure it would have been a terrible one. My mother loved it, though. Growing up in an office environment, I learned how to type, and actually typed it. I think down deep, I always imagined I'd one day become a famous writer. I'm still waiting!"

Chrysteen's career journey includes diverse experiences, from working at Capitol Records to running a family construction business. These varied roles have significantly shaped her writing and the themes she explores in her novels. "As with most authors, everything we do in life creates experiences; sometimes they're interesting enough to include in your writing. I've always loved old homes, and in my cabin series, my main character, Annie, is an interior designer. And that's how she meets several of the people who had ties to the cabins. She loves restoring cabins and I've enjoyed sharing some of the things she's done. I didn't use my experience at Capitol Records until I started working on Family Portrait which will be out next year."

Joining a writer's group with Elizabeth George in the 1980s had a profound impact on Chrysteen's writing style and her decision to return to writing after retiring from her business. "She and I were almost at the same stages of our writing when I met her, although she had a lot more discipline than I did, and went on to write wonderful stories for those many years before I got back into the swing of it."

The mountainous setting of Lake Arrowhead plays a significant role in Chrysteen's Cabin novels. "We loved the mountains and all the fresh crisp air. I couldn't help but think what a wonderful location to set my books in. When we finally retired, we combined our mountain home with our Long Beach home, and we kept a lot of our decor; as a designer, I was able to merge the mountain look with classic traditional decor, and my husband and I love it."

T*he Man in Cabin Number Five* features parallel stories of two women, Annie and Alyce. Chrysteen explains, "We had a second home in the mountains of Lake Arrowhead, California, and I still had a desire to write. I spent almost a year trying to figure out what I was going to write, and what my characters would do to sustain a series. Annie's story is loosely based on me when I got a divorce many years ago, and I actually used part of my husband's childhood experiences for Alyce."

Chrysteen's *Guest Book Trilogy* blends historical fiction, romance, and mystery. She shares, "I'll never be an author who sticks with one genre. I knew I didn't necessarily want a happily ever after ending, and I wanted to add some mystery and intrigue about people who 'stayed in the cabins'. I'm not a 'true' historical fiction author, basing my story on events from a specific time/era, but I do include a lot of history and facts about the mountains in my writing."

Chrysteen Braun's journey is a testament to the enduring power of passion and perseverance. Her diverse experiences and rich life story continue to inspire her writing, captivating readers with every novel she pens.

> **"**
> *As with most authors, everything we do in life creates experiences; sometimes they're interesting enough to include in your writing. I've always loved old homes, and in my cabin series, my main character, Annie, is an interior designer. And that's how she meets several of the people who had ties to the cabins.*

Chrysteen Braun

The Mischief-Maker of Modern Literature

G. S. Gerry, an award-winning author, discusses his humorous and satirical writing process, the creation of the Humour Den, and the personal experiences inspiring his unique narratives.

Exploring Life's Absurdities with Wit and Charm

G. S. Gerry, an award-winning author, has carved a niche for himself in the literary world by infusing humor, satire, and captivating narratives into his work. Known for his ability to transform ordinary situations into extraordinary tales, Gerry's books leave readers laughing and reflecting on life's absurdities. His diverse background—ranging from book bindery to military service to cybersecurity expertise—adds depth to his storytelling, making each book a unique blend of wit, charm, and unforgettable moments. With multiple awards and Amazon #1 Best Sellers, Gerry's work transcends genres and captures the imaginations of readers globally.

Gerry opens up about his creative journey, his unique approach to writing, and the inspirations behind his beloved works.

The Genesis of the Humour Den

When asked about the inspiration behind his blog, the Humour Den, Gerry explains, "It all started with a sprinkle of wit, a dash of sarcasm, and a pinch of absurdity. My aim was to create a space where readers could escape their everyday lives and dive headfirst into a world of laughter and reflection through my own real-life stories."

The Humour Den is an extension of the humor and charm found in Gerry's books. By sharing witty anecdotes, quirky observations, and humorous musings, he hopes to brighten readers' days and remind them to find joy in life's absurd moments. "Laughter is not just a luxury but a necessity," he says, emphasizing the importance of humor in everyday life.

Crafting Unique Narratives

Gerry's books, such as *Meth Murder & Amazon*" and "Hysterical Hangouts With The Hindlegs," blend humor with unexpected twists. Describing his creative process, Gerry reveals, "It all starts with a spark of inspiration—whether it's a quirky character, a bizarre situation, or even a random thought. From there, it's about letting the imagination run wild while keeping a firm grip on the reins of storytelling."

He balances humor and suspense by infusing his writing with witty dialogue, absurd situations, and quirky characters. "My goal is to keep readers guessing and leave them eagerly turning the pages to see what happens next," Gerry says, highlighting his commitment to entertaining and engaging his audience.

Family Dynamics and Personal Experiences

In "Hysterical Hangouts With The Hindlegs," family dynamics play a significant role. Gerry draws inspiration from personal experiences and observations to develop these characters and their interactions. "The story started from personal experiences of meeting my wife's family," he shares. "But I didn't want to make it a non-fiction story. I used those experiences as a catapult to take the reader on a hilarious journey."

Through creative liberties and a deep appreciation for the chaos and comedy of familial relationships, Gerry crafts a narrative that resonates with readers. The Hindlegs, while fictional, reflect the messy, marvelous world of family life, capturing the joy, absurdity, and unconditional love that comes with it.

Balancing Humor and Complexity

Gerry's writing style bridges comedy with originality, tackling sensitive or complex topics with a delicate balance. "Humor has a unique power to disarm, allowing readers to approach even the most sensitive topics with an open mind and a light heart," he explains. By staying true to the characters and their experiences, Gerry ensures that the humor arises organically from the story itself.

His approach to sensitive topics involves authenticity and empathy. "I use humor as a tool to explore, rather than diminish, their significance," he says. This balance creates narratives that entertain, enlighten, and leave readers both smiling and thoughtful.

Themes and Messages in "Meth Murder & Amazon"

"Meth Murder & Amazon" tackles intriguing themes like buying and selling, family dynamics, and unexpected twists. Gerry hopes readers take away a deeper understanding of human nature and the unpredictable nature of life itself. "Sometimes life really is stranger than fiction," he notes. Through the chaotic adventures of his characters, he aims to highlight the complexities of human relationships and the absurdities of the world.

Gerry's goal is to provoke thought and reflection while entertaining his audience. "If 'Meth Murder & Amazon' leaves readers pondering the intricacies of human relationships and perhaps even laughing in the face of adversity, then I'll consider my mission accomplished!"

The Birth of the Humour Den

The Humour Den's concept evolved from a catchy tune and an inside joke shared with his brother and sons. "My sons and brother used to sing this song, 'it's great then and then it's great then and then it's GREAT!' It always made me laugh and led me down the path of creating a play on that... From Great Then to the Humor Den."

This playful beginning blossomed into a blog where humor reigns supreme, celebrating life's absurdities. The Humour Den is a testament to the power of laughter, family, and the joy found in sharing a good joke with loved ones.

G. S. Gerry's unique blend of humor, satire, and captivating storytelling continues to leave an indelible mark on the literary world. Through his books and the Humour Den, he invites readers to laugh, ponder, and embark on unforgettable journeys, reminding us all that life is too short not to laugh—even in the face of complexity.

G. S. Gerry masterfully combines humor and heart, transforming everyday moments into captivating, laugh-out-loud stories that resonate deeply.

My creative process is a delicate dance between humor and suspense, laughter and intrigue. It's about taking readers on a rollercoaster ride of emotions, from belly laughs to nail-biting suspense, all while keeping them thoroughly entertained from start to finish."

G. S. Gerry

Toni Anderson discusses her transition from marine biology to writing, the influence of science on her novels, and the meticulous research behind her bestselling FBI Romantic Thrillers.

From Marine Biology to Bestselling Thrillers

TONI ANDERSON

CRAFTING AUTHENTIC FBI THRILLERS WITH HEART AND HEAT

AS TOLD TO DAN PETERS

Toni Anderson is a master of blending gritty suspense with steamy romance, captivating readers worldwide with her FBI Romantic Thrillers. A New York Times and USA Today bestselling author, Toni's journey from a small town in Shropshire, England, to the vast Canadian prairies is as fascinating as the stories she crafts. With a Ph.D. in Marine Biology, her path to becoming a celebrated author is a testament to her diverse talents and relentless pursuit of storytelling.

Toni's impressive achievements extend beyond her literary success. From mastering the Tokyo subway to surviving nineteen Winnipeg winters, her adventurous spirit fuels her writing. Her dedication to research has taken her to the heart of FBI operations in Washington, D.C., and the Writer's Police Academy in Wisconsin, ensuring her novels are as authentic as they are thrilling.

In this exclusive interview, Toni shares insights into her transition from science to writing, the influence of her scientific background on her novels, and the meticulous research behind her gripping stories. She also offers a glimpse into her latest release, *Cold Fury*, promising readers an emotional and exhilarating addition to the Cold Justice – Most Wanted series. Join us as we delve into the mind of a writer who continues to push the boundaries of romantic suspense.

I've always been a voracious reader and was bitten by the urge to write while doing my second post-doc. It took about a decade for me to learn my craft and to get traction in publishing, so I hope that gives any aspiring writers some encouragement. Not everyone is an overnight success.

As an author with a background in science, do you find yourself incorporating scientific elements or themes into your novels? If so, how does this influence your storytelling?

There was a horrible moment when an element I used in a story with snow leopards (The Killing Game) actually started to happen

---

Toni Anderson masterfully combines suspense and romance, creating compelling stories that captivate readers and earn critical acclaim worldwide.

---

with other endangered species. The telemetry devices used to study animals was being picked up by would-be poachers. Obviously, I wasn't the cause but that was a moment where my science background and storytelling collided dramatically.

I've certainly had several STEM heroines working within the sciences as characters in my books. I like to think I've helped banish the myth of the cold, logical scientist that I've read way too often over the years. Scientists can be messy and weird, grumpy and flawed, and beautiful and smart. Some of my earlier books had plots based on some of my own research projects but having moved onto the FBI there is less of that nowadays. I did use a poison dart frog and a frog biologist in one of my FBI books, so you never know when the science nerd will break through.

The Cold Justice series has been incredibly successful. What do you think draws readers to your brand of romantic thrillers, and how do you keep the series fresh and engaging with each new instalment?

I think it's the fact readers get both a fully fleshed suspense/thriller story combined with an emotionally satisfying romantic relationship that keeps my very loyal readers coming back for more, which I appreciate greatly. Aside from the fact my stories follow genre expectations (dangerous situations with characters in jeopardy, plus a romance) I try to write unique plots (as much as any plot is unique, ha!) which keeps things fresh. Readers also tell me they come back for the recurring characters who pop up in various stories.

Could you tell us more about the research process behind your novels, particularly those involving law enforcement and FBI operations? How do you ensure accuracy while still crafting a compelling narrative?

When I started out there was very little information available on the FBI and I did the best I could with the dearth of data I found in my small bedroom office back in Scotland. Since the internet exploded it's been a lot easier. The FBI now has a wonderful website and YouTube is an endless source of everything you never knew you needed to know. I've also been lucky enough to be able to get a tour of FBI headquarters in Washington, D.C., including the Strategic Information and Operations Center which is where all the James Bond type stuff happens. I also attended the Writers' Police Academy several times and would love to go again. So much good stuff happens there. Informative workshops, interaction with former detectives, FBI, Secret Service, DEA agents. Hands on experience with forensic anthropologists, psychologists, fingerprint, and blood collection evidence experts. I was thrilled to be allowed behind the wheel to perform a PIT maneuverer on a police patrol vehicle one year. Much of the research also comes from consuming autobiographies of former agents and watching documentaries. I do reserve the right to use artistic license in the pursuit of good fiction. I think the key to finding balance is only including the information pertinent to the story. No one wants to wade through an info dump of all the weird things you've been researching.

With the upcoming release of "Cold Fury," what can readers expect from this latest addition to the Cold Justice – Most Wanted series? Are there any new twists or characters we should be excited about?

COLD FURY is a pretty emotional book. It starts with a woman, an attorney, who has lost everything, so she obviously brings a lot of pain to the story. The hero is part of the FBI's Hostage Rescue Team but I gave him a science background that I borrowed from a friend to give him some extra special color. Cold Fury is a story about finding ways to forgive the mistakes of the past and move on. It's also a novel about a strong female character who isn't intimidated by the male dominated world of criminal justice system. In terms of characters, a reader favorite name of Lincoln Frazer, a profiler with the FBI's Behavioral Analysis Unit, decided he was going to have a lot to say in this book. I think that will make a lot of fans very happy.

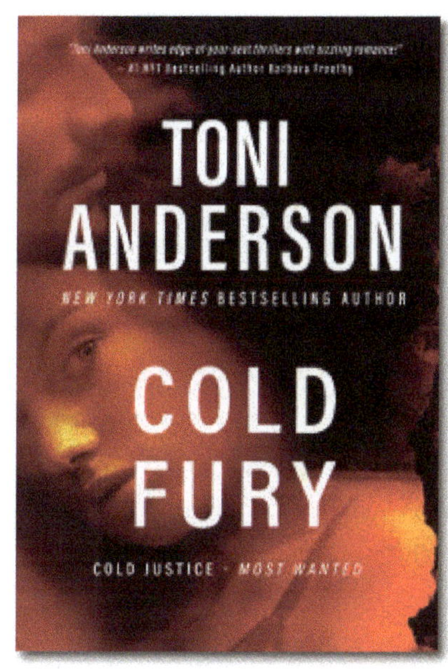

COLD FURY
by Toni Anderson

Cold Fury is a thrilling masterpiece, blending intense suspense and heartfelt romance, keeping readers captivated from start to finish.

Cold Fury: A Romantic Thriller by Toni Anderson is a gripping addition to the Cold Justice® - Most Wanted series that masterfully blends suspense, romance, and relentless action. The story centers on Hope Harper, a former star defense attorney whose life was shattered when a wrongfully released defendant murdered her family. Now an Assistant District Attorney, Hope is driven by a singular mission: to ensure that no other family suffers as hers did.

The plot thickens when the same serial killer escapes from a maximum-security prison during a brutal winter storm, setting his sights on revenge. Enter Aaron Nash, an FBI Hostage Rescue Team operator assigned to protect Hope. Despite her refusal to go into protective custody, Aaron is determined to keep her safe. Their initial friction gradually gives way to mutual respect and a burgeoning attraction, adding a layer of emotional depth to the high-stakes narrative.

Anderson's skillful storytelling keeps readers on the edge of their seats, weaving together intense action scenes with moments of poignant vulnerability. The chemistry between Hope and Aaron is palpable, and their evolving relationship adds a compelling dimension to the thriller. As the killer's rampage continues, the tension escalates, leading to a heart-pounding climax that will leave readers breathless.

Cold Fury is a must-read for fans of romantic thrillers, offering a perfect blend of danger, passion, and resilience. Toni Anderson delivers a powerful story of survival and second chances that will stay with you long after the final page.

Crafting Stories of Resilience and Renewal

Exploring Middle-Age Challenges and Personal Growth

Kirsten Pursell, an award-winning American author, has captivated readers with her deeply personal and emotionally resonant works. Her latest novel, *Long Enough to Love You*, released on January 1, 2023, delves into the challenges and new beginnings faced in middle age. This book, along with her previous works, has garnered significant acclaim, including several prestigious awards.

Pursell's journey as an author began with her memoir, *On Becoming Me: Memoir of an 80's Teenager,* published in 2021. This memoir, which reached #1 on Amazon's women's biographies and memoirs, offers a raw and unfiltered glimpse into her teenage years. Unlike typical reflective memoirs, Pursell's book is composed of her actual diary entries, journals, letters, and poetry from that era. "Writing the book was cathartic," she shares. "It's the evolution of a young girl into a woman, and it resonates with readers because it's a genuine account of growing up."

Her first novel, *Harvard*, blends elements of academia, athletics, and romance. The idea for the book came to her during a family trip, inspired by her love for running. "I envisioned two people crashing into each other on a mountain trail while running from their respective demons," she explains. The characters, Helena and Thor, developed organically, reflecting Pursell's approach to character creation.

In *Company Clown*, Pursell explores the world of advertising and corporate culture, drawing from her own experiences in product marketing for a major fast-food chain. Initially intended as a screenplay, the novel evolved into a satirical account of the rise of a corporate icon, inspired by a hand model she met at a commercial shoot. "I loved taking someone whose 'only' beauty was his hands and giving him center stage," she says.

Balancing her passions for competitive swimming and writing, Pursell finds parallels between the two disciplines. "Loving the process is a must for both," she notes. "Swimming has taught me discipline; writing has given me an outlet for expression. I need both in my life."

Pursell's books have achieved significant success, with *On Becoming Me* reaching #1 in women's biographies and memoirs. This success has encouraged her to continue writing, particularly stories featuring underrepresented middle-aged women protagonists. "It's motivating and encouraging to have readers become fans," she says. "I never thought I would be in that position."

Living in Ocean Beach, California, provides a rich backdrop for Pursell's creativity. "The ocean is mesmerizing, and Ocean Beach is full of quirky characters," she shares. "I get new ideas constantly." Her diverse literary portfolio, ranging from memoirs to poetry collections to novels, reflects her drive to explore varied genres and themes. "I write what inspires me," she says. "To limit myself to just women's fiction or romance means I can't explore other genres that excite me."

Kirsten Pursell's work continues to inspire and resonate with readers, offering stories

Harvard was the first novel I wrote. The idea came to me while driving down a mountain after a family weekend. As someone who loves to run, I had a vision of two people literally crashing into each other on a mountain trail while running from their respective demons. The characters have background stories that draw them together. Like most characters I write about, I have a general idea of who they are but let much of their story happen organically. (On a fun note, I wrote this book when my daughter, Quinne, was 12. She went on to graduate from Harvard nearly ten years later!)

Kirsten Pursell

Master of Dark Fantasy

Exploring the Craft of Character Development and Suspense in the Shards Trilogy and 'The Descendant'

BY DAN PETERS

Exploring the Craft of Character Development and Suspense

Acclaimed author Jason Gabriel, a resident of the Midwestern United States, has been a literary force ever since he first delved into the world of books with J.R.R. Tolkien's *Lord of the Rings*. This transformative experience ignited a passion for storytelling that has only grown stronger over the decades. Gabriel's novels are known for their intricate character arcs and richly detailed settings, and his latest work, *The Descendant,* is no exception. In this novel, a group of protagonists must confront their inner demons to face a looming threat to their world, a narrative approach that has resonated deeply with his readers.

Gabriel's fascination with damaged characters and their complex journeys is a hallmark of his writing. He skillfully uses these characters to create suspense, conflict, and tension, weaving them seamlessly into his narratives. This method is evident in his Shards Trilogy, particularly in the character of Brandt, a "*broken*" protagonist whose journey of overcoming personal demons serves as a powerful metaphor for transformation. Gabriel describes the trilogy as a "*roller coaster ride*," filled with the ups and downs of character development.

When asked about his writing process for crafting suspense and action in "The Hunt for the Descendant," Gabriel emphasizes the importance of character development. He begins with a series of "what if" questions to build his characters, allowing their arcs to drive the suspense in the story. He also employs "Character auditions," writing a few pages with a protagonist or antagonist to see if they fit into the narrative. This meticulous process ensures that each character contributes meaningfully to the story's tension and excitement.

Balancing fantasy and suspense is another critical aspect of Gabriel's storytelling. He strives to create a fantasy setting that feels real and engaging while maintaining a high level of conflict and suspense. This balance is crucial to keeping readers invested in the story and ensuring that the fantasy elements enhance rather than detract from the narrative.

Developing Brandt's character and his emotional journey posed significant challenges for Gabriel. Maintaining a character arc over three books requires careful pacing to keep readers engaged without rushing the character's development. Gabriel's solution is a delicate balancing act, ensuring that Brandt's progress is neither too fast nor too slow.

The Hunt for the Descendant sets the stage for the rest of the Shards Trilogy, with books two and three promising to escalate the tension and suspense. Gabriel hints at the introduction of a new female protagonist in the upcoming books, a character he is particularly excited about. This new addition is expected to bring fresh dynamics to the story and further enrich the narrative.

In Gabriel's view, a compelling dark fantasy novel requires high stakes, relentless suspense, and characters that readers care about, all set within a dangerous fantasy world. He achieves this by creating characters whose fates matter deeply to him, even when their primary purpose is to die. This emotional investment in his characters translates into a gripping and immersive reading experience for his audience.

When not writing, Gabriel enjoys riding his bike through the scenic woods near his home and cherishes time spent with his family. His dedication to his craft and his ability to create deeply engaging stories make him a standout author in the realm of dark fantasy.

Gabriel's commitment to his readers is evident in every page he writes. He meticulously crafts each character, ensuring they are multi-dimensional and relatable. This attention to detail extends to his world-building, where he creates settings that are not only fantastical but also grounded in reality. This duality allows readers to lose themselves in his books while still feeling a connection to the world he has created.

The positive response from readers to *The Descendant,* is a testament to Gabriel's skill as a storyteller. His ability to blend complex characters with a richly detailed setting has created a novel that is both thrilling and thought-provoking. As readers eagerly await the next installments in the Shards Trilogy, it is clear that Jason Gabriel's work will continue to captivate and inspire.

Jason Gabriel's journey from a young reader enchanted by "Lord of the Rings" to an acclaimed author of dark fantasy is a story of passion, dedication, and talent. His ability to create compelling characters and immersive worlds has earned him a devoted following and a place among the greats in the genre. With more exciting works on the horizon, Gabriel's star is sure to continue rising.

> *I am very cautious about the fantasy elements in my books. I make certain that the fantasy setting makes sense and feels real. Hopefully, the readers will feel the same. I want it to be exciting, different, and interesting, but I try to maintain a balance so it feels real.*

Jason Gabriel

A true literary talent

J.T. Ellison, a bestselling author and Emmy® Award-winning TV host, shares her journey from politics to writing, exploring dark themes, co-authoring, and her love for fantasy.

The Journey of a Bestselling Author and Emmy® Award-Winning TV Host

New York Times & USA Today's Bestselling Author

J.T. Ellison masterfully blends suspense and character depth, captivating readers with her thrilling narratives and versatile storytelling.

J.T. Ellison, the New York Times and USA Today bestselling author, has captivated readers with over 30 critically acclaimed novels. Her impressive repertoire includes standalone thrillers like *A Very Bad Thing*, *It's One of U*s, and *Her Dark Lies*, as well as series such as the Lt. Taylor Jackson and Dr. Samantha Owens series. Ellison's collaboration with #1 New York Times bestselling author Catherine Coulter on the "A Brit in the FBI" series further solidified her status in the literary world. Beyond her novels, she is also the Emmy® Award-winning co-host of the television series *A Word on Words*.

Ellison's journey to becoming a bestselling author is as fascinating as her novels. After moving to Nashville and struggling to find a job, a librarian introduced her to John Sandford's Prey series. This encounter sparked her decision to write, leading to the creation of her iconic character, Taylor Jackson. Ellison credits her political background for instilling in her the discipline necessary for writing. "The political world taught me one very important trait: discipline," she explains. This discipline has been a cornerstone of her successful transition from politics to writing.

Ellison's novels delve into dark and thrilling themes, exploring crime, suspense, and psychological tension. She is drawn to these themes by a fascination with human behavior and a desire to see justice served. "I am fascinated by how terrible people can be to one another, and I like to see justice served in some way," she says. This fascination drives her to create complex characters and intricate plots that keep readers on the edge of their seats.

In addition to her solo work, Ellison has co-authored a successful series with Catherine Coulter. The collaboration process, while challenging, has been immensely rewarding for her. "Cowriting is a lot of fun and can also be hugely challenging," she notes. The synergy between the two authors, combined with their shared work ethic, has resulted in a series that has captivated readers worldwide.

Ellison also writes contemporary fantasy under the pen name Joss Walker. This genre switch allows her to explore new creative freedoms. "Fantasy is my one true love right now, mostly because if you get into a bind…magic!" she exclaims. The ability to conjure solutions and build expansive worlds offers a refreshing contrast to the constraints of thriller writing.

As the co-host of *A Word on Words*, Ellison has had the opportunity to broaden her literary horizons. Hosting the show has allowed her to explore diverse genres and voices, enriching her own writing. One of her most memorable moments on the show was being locked in a jail cell with Margaret Atwood. "She was such a good sport," Ellison recalls with a smile.

Ellison's diverse background, from growing up in rural Colorado to working in high-stakes political environments, has significantly influenced her writing. Her settings often reflect her varied experiences, with Nashville serving as a central backdrop in many of her novels. She also draws inspiration from her travels, with the UK, France, and Italy featuring prominently in her stories.

J.T. Ellison's journey from the political arena to the literary world is a testament to her versatility and dedication. Her ability to weave intricate plots, create compelling characters, and explore dark themes has earned her a loyal readership and critical acclaim. As she continues to write and explore new genres, readers can look forward to more thrilling and imaginative stories from this talented author.

J.T. Ellison lives in Nashville with her husband and twin kittens, one of whom is a ghost. She is currently hard at work on her next novel, continuing to captivate readers with her unique blend of suspense, intrigue, and creativity.

> *I am fascinated by how terrible people can be to one another, and I like to see justice served in some way. Too often, cases go unsolved and families are torn apart. When I write thrillers, I'm always imagining what's happening on the other side of the door. If it's a procedural, my character knocks on the doors. If it's suspense, the character's door is knocked upon. It gives me a deeper perspective on the emotional frailty of the characters.*

J.T. Ellison

The Heart and Soul of Small-Town Mysteries

Katherine H. Klemp, a retired nurse and mother, channels her life experiences into her Eagle River Detectives series, blending emotional depth with small-town adventures for young readers.

BY DAN PETERS

Exploring the Emotional Depth and Adventure in The Eagle River Detectives Series

Katherine H. Klemp, a mother of eight and grandmother to many, has seamlessly transitioned from a career in nursing to becoming an acclaimed author. Her children, lively and curious, bear a striking resemblance to the Grant kids in her popular series, *The Eagle River Detectives*. Katherine's professional background as a registered nurse, particularly her work with the elderly and her leadership in grief programs, has profoundly influenced the emotional depth and themes in her writing. Now residing in White Bear Township, MN, Katherine continues to share her love for storytelling and God's word with readers of all ages.

Katherine's experiences in nursing and grief counseling have significantly shaped her fiction. In the first book of *The Eagle River Detectives* series, the Grant children grapple with the loss of their father and their grandfather's memory issues. These themes of loss and coping are drawn from Katherine's real-life experiences, offering young readers a blueprint for dealing with similar situations in their own lives. The series not only entertains but also educates, providing a gentle guide for children facing grief and change.

The lively and curious nature of the Grant kids is a direct reflection of Katherine's own children. Her son, Peter, once remarked that reading the first book felt like reliving his childhood. Katherine's stories are peppered with inside jokes and anecdotes from her family life, making the series a personal and engaging read for those who know her well.

Writing under different pen names for her fiction and non-fiction works, Katherine navigates the creative process with ease. Fiction allows her the freedom to create and explore new worlds, often surprising herself with the twists and turns of her plots. In contrast, her non-fiction work is grounded in truth, yet she approaches it with the same storytelling passion. Her understanding of the grieving process, for instance, enriches her fiction, allowing her to portray the Grant children's sadness and resilience authentically.

The setting of Eagle River, with its vivid small-town atmosphere, is inspired by Katherine's own experiences in Seward, Nebraska. This charming town, with its manufacturing plant, swimming pool, and vibrant 4th of July celebrations, serves as the perfect backdrop for the adventures of the Eagle River detectives. Katherine's love for small-town life shines through in her detailed and affectionate portrayal of Eagle River.

Katherine's inspiration for writing detective stories for younger readers stemmed from a book fair at her grandchildren's school. Disappointed by the lack of child heroes in the available books, she decided to create her own series where kids take center stage. Influenced by her childhood favorites, Nancy Drew and the Boxcar Children, Katherine crafted stories that appeal to both young readers and older generations. Her books offer a nostalgic journey for adults while providing thrilling adventures for children.

Balancing the revelation of secrets throughout *The Grant Legacy* series is a delicate task. Katherine ensures that each book can stand alone while maintaining a continuous thread of suspense and mystery. With the help of her high school friend, Jan Hughes, who creates activity sheets for each book, Katherine keeps readers engaged without giving away too much too soon. The goal is always to keep the reader turning pages, eager to uncover the next secret.

Katherine H. Klemp's journey from nursing to novelist is a testament to her versatility and passion for storytelling. Her rich life experiences, combined with her love for adventure and mystery, have resulted in a series that resonates with readers of all ages. Through her books, Katherine continues to touch lives, offering both entertainment and valuable life lessons.

> " *I started writing these books after attending a book fair at my grandchildren's school and couldn't find any books where kids were the heroes. Mostly animals or imaginary characters saved the day. The book closest to the theme I wanted was, Barbie Saves Camp, and Barbie is neither a child nor a real person!*
>
> *The adventure and mystery came from a deep love for Nancy Drew books and the stories of the Boxcar children I read as a child. I find that my audience is the young and the old. The 9–14-year-olds, and the 60–90-year-olds. Kids still love adventure, and many of my contemporaries enjoy reliving our small-town childhoods.*"

Katherine H. Klemp

Weaving Love and Adventure in Every Tale

Wendy Zuccarello blends her veterinary background and personal experiences to create heartfelt novels that explore love, forgiveness, and personal growth, set against the beautiful backdrop of Maine.

BY Z. ROBERTS

Advice and Insights from a Celebrated Indie Author

Wendy Zuccarello, an acclaimed author with a BS in Animal Science and an MFA in Creative Writing, has carved a unique niche in the literary world. Known for her contemporary romance, romantic suspense, and dystopian novels, Zuccarello's work is a testament to her diverse interests and rich life experiences. Married to her high school sweetheart for twenty years, she is a proud mother of two teenagers and a devoted caretaker of numerous pets. Her career in the veterinary industry, spanning two decades, has provided her with a wealth of experiences, from treating hamsters to hippos, which she skillfully weaves into her narratives.

Zuccarello's novels are deeply rooted in themes of love, forgiveness, and personal growth. She believes that relationships are complex and multifaceted, often filled with challenges and unexpected turns. "Happily ever afters are amazing, but the journey there is often filled with bumps, unexpected turns, and immense challenges," she explains. Her stories reflect this belief, emphasizing the importance of the journey as much as the outcome. Drawing heavily from personal experiences, Zuccarello strives to tell stories that resonate with authenticity and emotional depth.

Her background in animal science and veterinary technology uniquely informs her writing. Animals play significant roles in her books, reflecting their importance in people's lives. One of her favorite works, "Never Let Go," features a protagonist who is a penguin keeper at an aquarium, a role inspired by Zuccarello's own experiences. She fondly recalls incorporating true stories from her time working with African Penguins into the narrative. Additionally, her books often feature dogs and even a chipmunk, inspired by Munchkin, a chipmunk she hand-feeds in her backyard.

In "Loudening Silence," Zuccarello introduces a protagonist who is deaf, adding a layer of diversity and representation to her storytelling. This novel is particularly meaningful to her, as both of her teenagers are hearing impaired. Their experiences and resilience inspired her to create a story that accurately portrays the challenges and triumphs of living with hearing impairment. Dedicated to her children, Kaitlyn and AJ, the book includes the touching story of Kaitlyn receiving her hearing aids for the first time.

The "Healing Mountain Series" delves into the complexities of relationships and the journey towards forgiveness. Zuccarello emphasizes the significance of forgiveness, describing it as a path to peace and inner strength. "Forgiveness is a difficult concept in so many situations. It is about finding peace and inner strength," she says. The series, based partly on her personal experiences, aims to convey that while struggling is natural, it is crucial not to let it hinder personal growth and healing.

Maine, a state that holds a special place in Zuccarello's heart, serves as the backdrop for some of her novels. Her love for Maine began in high school and has only deepened over the years. The state's beauty, peace, and simplicity provide the perfect setting for her stories. A memorable trip to Acadia National Park with her daughter further solidified her connection to Maine, making it an integral part of her storytelling.

As a self-published author, Zuccarello finds immense satisfaction in holding a book she wrote in her hands. The journey of self-publishing, while challenging, offers her complete control over her work. She advises aspiring authors to persevere, write what they love, and give it their all. "Never give up. Write what you love. Give it your all. Don't look back," she encourages. Importantly, she reminds indie authors that their success is not defined by sales but by the passion and dedication they pour into their work.

Wendy Zuccarello's journey as an author is a testament to her resilience, creativity, and unwavering love for storytelling. Her books, rich with authentic experiences and heartfelt themes, continue to captivate readers, offering them a glimpse into the complexities of love, forgiveness, and personal growth.

> " *Relationships are not always easy, and there are so many things in life that can impact them. I have always wanted to reflect this in my writing. Happily, ever after are amazing, but the journey there is often filled with bumps, unexpected turns, and immense challenges. There is so much more to the classic "boy meets girl; boy and girl fall in love; boy and girl live happily ever after," and that is what I write. The journey is by far just as important as the outcome. My writing is heavily influenced by personal experience, and I strive to tell stories that are real."*

Wendy Zuccarello

Weaving Faith and Fantasy

L. M. Montes blends her educational background and love for fantasy to create Christian urban fantasy

L. M. Montes, an acclaimed author known for her Christian urban fantasy novels, short stories, and poetry, has carved a unique niche in the literary world. With a background in education and English, and an extensive academic portfolio that includes two master's degrees, Montes has seamlessly blended her love for the fantastical with her passion for teaching. Her works, including *The Veil of Time* and *The Cross's Key*, reflect a deep intertwining of supernatural elements and real-world settings, offering readers a thought-provoking and enjoyable experience.

Montes's journey into writing was significantly influenced by her teaching career and real-life experiences. She explains, "My teaching experience in the classroom years ago and other real-life experiences opened the door to writing novels and poetry using teaching elements within them by way of the themes found throughout my writings." This blend of education and fantasy allows her to dig deeper within

herself, creating stories that not only entertain but also convey life's lessons in a joyful manner.

Her foray into Christian urban fantasy was somewhat serendipitous. Initially setting out to write a romance novel, Montes's creative writing professor suggested adding a fantasy element. This suggestion ignited a spark, leading her to explore the genre further. "Incorporating faith into my storytelling comes from wanting to share the love of Christ with others but doing it in such a way that readers will find it thought-provoking and enjoyable at the same time," she says. Montes carefully selects scriptures that align with her storylines, ensuring that her characters' arcs reflect spiritual growth and resilience.

In her *Time* series, Montes's protagonist, Tora, embarks on a journey of self-discovery, facing formidable adversaries and internal conflicts. Montes delves into themes of identity and overcoming darkness, portraying Tora as a strong-willed character who gradually realizes the strength in seeking help. "She now understands that, when the darkness beckons her, she finds her own strengths are not enough," Montes explains, highlighting the importance of community and faith in overcoming challenges.

Montes's collection of short stories, *Lights of Fantasy,* showcases her versatility as a writer. Drawn to genres like fantasy, mystery, and intrigue, she enjoys the thrill these stories provide. Crafting short fiction, however, requires a different approach compared to longer works. Montes focuses on developing a single idea with a concise conclusion, often jotting down additional ideas for future novels. For her longer works, she employs a meticulous process involving binders, journals, and detailed notes to manage complex plots and character development.

Beyond writing, Montes engages in creative pursuits like blogging and creating beaded jewelry. These activities complement her writing process, often serving as sources of inspiration. "The adoration of jewelry and all that sparkles within it is responsible for the inspiration of my first book, *The Veil of Time*," she reveals. Her blog not only promotes her books but also serves as a platform to teach others about the writing process.

Montes's literary journey has been enriched by her features in Canvas Rebel Magazine and interviews on platforms like The Neil Haley Show. These experiences have reinvigorated her passion for writing, especially during times of self-doubt. Her advice to aspiring writers is simple yet profound: "Never give up. Share your work." Montes's story is a testament to the power of perseverance and the joy of sharing one's creative endeavors with the world.

L. M. Montes is a literary virtuoso, seamlessly weaving faith, fantasy, and introspection into captivating narratives that resonate with readers.

> *When crafting short fiction, I stick to one small idea and develop it with a short range or conclusion in mind. I keep the story on a 'leash' so to speak. That can be difficult at times when I am writing and the ideas start to flow to the point where I want to develop more, but I stick to the predetermined goal of keeping it short and write down any ideas for future use should I decide to turn any of them into full length novels."*

L. M. Montes

Available in
PRINT

Americas to Australia Europe to Africa Reader's House is available over 190 countries and thousands of retaiers, platforms including Amazon, Barnes & Noble, Walmart, Waterstone's .....

ELECTRONIC

It is an electronic (flip book) format and interactive. Accessable from electronic devices like pc, smart phone, notepads..

ONLINE

All interviews, we conduct make them accessable online for free.

SOCIAL MEDIA

We are on Facebook, Instagram and X. Please follow us on social media @novelistpost

contact us today for an interview opportunity at
editor@novelistpost.com

Save up to 50% when you order 10 or more from the same issue

<table>
<tr><td rowspan="2">Subscribe Now!</td><td colspan="2">

YES! I would like a subscription to

☐ Current Issue for

☐ One-Year Subscription (_______ Issues) for

☐ Two-Year Subscription (_______ Issues) for

    ☐ I am a renewing a current subscription   ☐ I am a new subscriber

Name: ________________________________ Phone: ________________

Shipping Address: _______________________________________

Billing Address: _______________________________________

Email: _______________________________________

    ☐ Yes, I would like to receive updates, newsletters and special offers

    ☐ No, I would NOT like to receive updates, newsletters and special offers

Payment Type: ☐ Check   ☐ Bank transfer   ☐ Wise   ☐ PayPal

____

____

Please mail this form to:
Magazine Name:
</td></tr>
</table>